Relic II
Resurrection

Relic II
Resurrection

Jonathan Brookes

Text copyright © 2015 Michael J. Polia, AB1AW

Layout and formatting by Cheryl D. Polia

Cover design by SelfPubBookCovers.com/Valdux

Cover illustration copyright © 2015 SelfPubBookCovers.com/Valdux

All rights reserved

First edition: October 2015

ISBN: 1517273048
ISBN-13: 978-1517273040

Dedicated to yin and yang, harmony, and balance;
all of which are sorely lacking in this book.

We choose what is right, and what is illusion.

TIMELINE

FOREWORD

It is a heady honor to be the seed for a story as exciting as Relic II. I never expected to be thrust into the dying ashes of a covert military project. It certainly hadn't been my first choice for achieving my fifteen minutes of fame. The chances of someone like me accidently running into a rogue like Jonathan Brookes are infinitesimal. For whatever reason, fate chose me.

It happened during a southbound trek on the Appalachian Trail. After two solid days of rain, the incessant cold and pain in my calves had been enough for me. My buddies and I had descended to and collapsed into the Melville Nauheim Shelter near Bennington, VT. Cold, wet, tired, sore, and at my limit, I willed myself to hike out the extra 1.5 miles to spend the night at a small inn across from Big Pond on Route 9. Staying there was like heaven compared to the shelter's less than spartan accommodations.

The next morning I slipped back into the woods just as the sun was coming up. A hot shower and my first night's sleep in a bed in a week had given me new energy and enthusiasm to continue the hike. It was good to see the sun again.

The trail back to the shelter was mostly uphill. The thick canopy of trees kept things dark and moist, sometimes slippery. At the steepest part of the ascent, I picked my way between thick, gnarled roots and exposed rocks, choosing my footing carefully so as not to slip and aggravate my already-achy calves. That is when fate intervened and Jonathan Brookes entered my life.

I heard a sharp yelp. I panicked, immediately thinking coyote, or worse. Unsure of the direction the sound came from, I stopped my climb, held my breath, listened carefully, and waited. A burst of profanity followed; clearly not a coyote. Curious, I took a few careful steps off the trail, peered between the trees, and spied a man lying face up in the brush.

Thinking that the man might have been injured, I relaxed and moved toward him. My heavy footsteps caught his attention. He twisted around to face me. The wide eyes of his bearded, rough-hewn face held the frightened look of a hunted man. He was grasping his leg. That's when I saw it. The shaft of an arrow was embedded in his thigh. A jagged patch of blood stained his denims.

I moved closer to help, but he immediately began waving me away. I figured he was accidently shot by a hunter and that he was concerned for my safety. It wasn't hunting season, but that never stopped some folks. Plus, given the way he was dressed, with dark blue jeans and a coffee-color plaid shirt, he certainly could have been mistaken for prey.

As I kept moving closer he must have realized that I was not going to leave him alone; he put a finger to his lips and motioned for me to crouch down. I knelt beside him, whipped off my backpack, and rummaged for something to staunch his bleeding. He grabbed my arm, stopping my search. He pressed a USB stick into my palm, and then insisted, in no uncertain terms, that I leave him immediately. Although I protested, his threatening tone and piercing stare made his intentions clear. My gut said, "Run!"

And run I did. I grabbed my backpack and hightailed it back to the inn where I had spent the night.

Two maintenance workers from the inn accompanied me back into the woods. I found the spot where I had found Brookes, but he was gone. The brush was badly torn, as if there had been a struggle. We searched the area but could find no sign of the man. He had disappeared.

The local authorities were summoned. I was thoroughly questioned and asked to remain in town. My southbound hike ruined, I stayed at the Inn for two days while various small search parties combed the woods. Nothing. It was as if I had made the whole thing up, something the county sheriff seemed more and more likely to believe.

I picked up a rental car in Bennington and drove to meet my buddies at the planned exit point. I had a story to tell!

Back home, I emptied the contents of my backpack. In the outside zipper pocket, I found the thumb drive; somehow it got shoved in there during all the excitement and forgotten until now.

Although wary of computer viruses, my curiosity got the best of me. I shoved the device into my laptop's USB port. The drive contained dozens of folders holding documents about a military conspiracy, cloning, an experiment gone bad; and something about Neanderthals.

One of the folders held a single photograph; two men, one dressed in a military uniform, the other in business attire. The man in the suit was holding a tiny infant. I did not recognize any of them.

As I continued reading through the documents, I realized there was something vaguely familiar about the information. A quick Google search yielded the results I needed. Brookes' story had been told before, as a novel, after a writer named Michael Polia had a similar encounter with the elusive whistle-blower a couple of years before.

I contacted Mr. Polia. He was skeptical until I put the thumb drive in his hands. The result of our meeting is the book you are about to read.

Is it true? I'll let you decide.

Brian Castelli
September, 2015

ACKNOWLEDGMENTS

My sincere thanks and appreciation to all the folks who helped me with critiques, editing, beta-reading, and the multitude of other unseen but necessary work and effort that goes into creating a novel.

First, no amount of thanks is sufficient for Mr. Brian Castelli, who risked life and limb to get the truth behind this story to a writer who could spin fact into fiction.

Special thanks to author Loren Schechter who contributed to the editing of this novel from the very first chapter.

Thanks also to authors Robert Cage, Shannon Hollinger, Gregory Lamb, and Jeffery Moore for the innumerable critiques, comments and corrections to the draft manuscripts.

A lot of eyes and red pens have seen and touched the various manuscript revisions over the course of writing this work. My thanks to all the talented and gifted writers at *The Wayland Writers Group* and *The Writers' Table critique sessions*. Your feedback and encouragement was crucial to completing this book.

Finally, I want to thank my beta-readers, Scott Hill, David Kassay, and author Jeff Suwak. Your reader's perspective helped determine what really worked and what was fluff.

RELIC II
RESURRECTION

SATURDAY, 2:37 PM MDT

"Stay on his ass, dammit! You're going to lose him in all this traffic!"

Colonel John Birchwood shouted orders to his taxi driver while keeping his eyes fixed on the black limo they were tailing. They bounced through a couple of intersections, nearly running a red light as the taxi driver swerved and dodged the unusually heavy weekend traffic in downtown Rapid City.

Birchwood jabbed a finger toward the limo as it pulled away from the rattling taxi.

"There! It's heading to the hospital entrance."

The limo coasted to a stop. Birchwood's taxi ground to a halt a car-length behind it. Without taking his eyes off the vehicle in front of them, Birchwood handed the cabbie a fifty and told him to wait. The limo sat by the curb for a few minutes without any activity. Birchwood checked his watch.

Eventually, the chauffeur emerged from the vehicle, sprinted around to a curbside passenger door and swung it open. A woman's leg appeared. Then the other. The two feet, clad in neon pink running shoes, planted themselves on the pavement. The chauffeur bent and reached out to offer a helping hand to the unseen passenger. The legs slid out further, followed by a distended belly clothed in an earth-toned dress that was bunched up around the woman's thighs.

Birchwood bounced his right fist on his thigh as he watched the woman's slow motion exit.

Come on. You're not that fat. Get on your feet you lazy civilian. You think the women giving birth in the Hindu Kush Mountains of Afghanistan have it this easy?

"How much longer?" The question came from the scraggly-faced cabbie. He drummed his fingers on the steering wheel and nodded his head to some silent rhythm.

Without turning his head, Birchwood threw him another fifty. "Shut up and sit still."

The driver retrieved the bill from the floor, then crossed his arms and stared out the window at the passing traffic.

Birchwood's patience was rewarded. A very pregnant young lady emerged from the limo and tottered at the edge of the curb. The chauffeur had her by the arm. He slung her bulging overnight bag over his shoulder. Birchwood rolled his eyes.

Christ, woman, you're not staying for a whole week.

He watched the chauffeur assist the woman as she trudged toward the hospital's main entrance.

When the pair got about halfway, Birchwood flung open his door. "Get lost," he barked at the cabbie and slammed the door closed behind him. The vehicle's tires screeched as the taxi sped away.

Despite the constant flow of pedestrians, Birchwood kept his eyes locked on his quarry. She and the chauffeur moved at a glacial pace towards the revolving doors.

Idiot. You're not going to make it through there.

As if on cue, the helpful coachman pointed towards a set of glass doors held wide open by a woman dressed far too elegantly for the Colonel to imagine her delivering a TV newscast, much less a baby.

"Julie!" Miss Elegance shouted and waved. "Julie, over here."

Birchwood spotted a wheelchair speeding from the open door, pushed by a lanky young man in blue scrubs.

That's it. Move it. Get her off her feet before she falls on her face.

Before the wheelchair could be positioned, Julie doubled over and vomited onto the chauffeur's black polished shoes.

Birchwood snorted to himself.

No good deed goes unpunished.

The elegant woman in high heels marched towards the mishap, barking orders to the attendant struggling to lift Julie from the sidewalk into the waiting wheelchair. She yanked the overnight bag from the hapless driver, shoved some cash into his hand, and strode back to hold open the hospital door, all the while shouting commands at the youth hustling Julie and the wheelchair into the hospital lobby.

Birchwood marched over to the unfortunate coachman fruitlessly wiping vomit off his shoes with a wad of newspaper. He shoved a hundred dollar bill in the driver's face and demanded, "Tell me everything, and I mean everything, that you know about that pregnant woman."

SATURDAY, 4:37 PM EDT

If only I could take a chainsaw to them!

General Holbrooke stood at his office window, muttering to himself about the view. A thick cloud of cigar smoke hung above his bald head.

Outside, the morning sun was pushing its way through the dense stand of Pitch pines that surrounded the newly built genome research facility. The gleaming glass structure's mirrored surfaces perfectly reflected the natural environment in which it was nestled, making the facility difficult to spot by any intrepid hiker exploring the Ridge-and-Valley Appalachians along the Clinch River.

Holbrooke found the view stifling. He preferred the vast horizon of the Dakota Badlands where the previous research facility was located. That secretive lab now lay in ruins, giving Holbrooke limited choices. The genomic facilities here at Oak Ridge were his only viable option to get his project back on track.

Damn shame we had to blow up the desert facility. I'm putting that on Summerston's head. If he had kept his nose to his work, we'd be a lot further along right now. At least we managed to salvage some of the frozen 'Thal embryos, so we're not starting from scratch.

He was confident that the project could get back on track faster here than at a reconstituted F&G. The former military contracting firm had been brought to its knees by an FBI raid last year. Someone had leaked info about Farnsworth & Grayson LLC being involved in an illegal surrogate adoption program involving prostitutes.

Serves those traitors at F&G right. They weren't supposed to be implanting any embryos. Heck, they weren't even supposed to have any viable embryos.

All the company's high level officers and directors had been arrested. However, one of the company's founders, Thomas Grayson, and his minion Doctor Bowers had somehow slipped away during the raid of the company's headquarters. Together, they had enough connections, knowledge, and money to rekindle the project on their own. They needed only enough viable genetic material to impregnate a single surrogate.

They'll never get their hands on any of it. Professor Carmichael is long dead and cremated. Summerton's dead or missing. We never did find his body after the explosion at the lab. Even if he was alive, he'd never cooperate with them.

The only remaining loose end is this fourth surrogate, Julie. How did she manage to drop off the grid during her pregnancy? She can't stay off the grid, though. She's going have to give birth at some hospital. There's no way she's going to risk a home delivery, not with the symptoms and complications she should be experiencing.

His office phone chirped on the desk behind him.

I've got to get me a real phone. One that has a real ring to it and doesn't sound like a drowning chipmunk.

His fat fingers jammed the lit end of his cigar stub into a chipped glass ashtray and grabbed the phone's handset. He cleared some phlegm from his throat, allowing his gravel-laden voice to growl. "Holbrooke."

A flat, disembodied voice announced itself. "Captain Robert Gordon, reporting, sir."

"Status."

"We've located Julie, sir. She's in Rapid City, South Dakota."

"I know what state Rapid City is in, Captain. Damn it! That's where F&G headquarters was located. In fact, it's where you and Lieutenant Sullivan are stationed. Are you telling me that she's been right under our noses all this time? What the hell is she doing there? Why isn't she in Sioux Falls with the other three surrogates?" Holbrooke thought for a moment. "She's not colluding with Grayson or Bowers, is she?"

"I don't believe so, sir. There's no way that she knows about the true nature of the child she's carrying. She's originally from here and returned to see her doctor for the remainder of the pregnancy. She'll probably give birth here."

"Intercept her before that happens. That child needs to be born in a military facility with the proper medical staff, and to assure that we have jurisdiction and custody of it."

"Yes sir. Lieutenant Sullivan had explained that to me back when we posed as the surrogate parents.

If Julie gives birth on federal military property, the state laws for adoption and surrogacy don't apply."

"How do you plan to acquire her and the child, Captain?"

"My plan is for me and Lieutenant Sullivan to make contact with Julie using our previous surrogate parent aliases. Julie knows us in that role."

Holbrooke rolled his eyes. "Lieutenant Sullivan's a smart attorney, but she's not field-ops material. She's not trained for this sort of mission, and her mental state has been under scrutiny this past year. I've read her psych profile. She's fit for desk duty, that's it."

"Sir, I'm not certain that I can complete this mission successfully alone, posing as a single parent looking to adopt a child."

"Lieutenant Walker is available to complete the mission with you."

"Lieutenant Craig Walker, sir? I don't understand."

"You're to use the alternate mission profile."

"The gay couple aliases, sir?"

"Yes, with Lieutenant Walker. He's stationed there in Rapid City. At Ellsworth Air Force Base. I want you and Walker to pose as an affluent, socially-conscious gay couple looking to adopt their first child. This surrogate must have figured out by now that the original couple she contracted with is not coming back. She's going to think that you and Sullivan skipped out on her. She'll want another couple to step in, cover the rest of her medical expenses and adopt the baby. She won't be able to resist making a social statement in the process.

"Please, sir, not Walker. I know Walker. I think he really is gay."

"Then he's perfect for the mission. Hell, we let them in, let's make use of them. People are sympathetic to their kind. They fawn all over them."

"Julie may recognize me from when Mary, I mean from when the Lieutenant and I interviewed her last year."

"Then get a haircut. Have Walker choose what you wear. You're not posing as the original couple that this surrogate met, only as a couple wanting to adopt a child. This surrogate is not keeping that baby. Is that clear? You need to convince her of that."

"Yes, sir. And Lieutenant Sullivan? She's eager to get some field experience."

The General fired back. "Lieutenant Sullivan is your legal consultant only. I don't want her in the field. You remember what happened last year. Summerston and Birchwood really screwed us over. One of them leaked top secret project info. The other one went nutty and destroyed all our data. Then the whole project got screwed up when the desert lab facility was discovered. You and Walker can get this project back on track by finding this girl and getting that child."

Holbrooke coughed and cleared a bit more phlegm from his throat. "Keep Sullivan on a short leash. I don't need another loose cannon screwing up this project."

"Yes, sir. I have Lieutenant Sullivan convinced that the entire project is scrubbed. She thinks I'm only cleaning up loose ends and that the infant is being rescued to save it from Birchwood. She has no idea about Oak Ridge."

"Good. She was getting too emotionally attached."

"Yes, I agree. I know you had that concern from the start, sir. My initial assessment of her was incorrect. But in some ways, Birchwood going rogue has made it easier to keep the Lieutenant in check. Her instincts are to protect the baby. I am using that to my advantage."

"Keep her out of the field. And keep yourself in check too, Captain. She's an asset and not a piece of ass." General Holbrooke's voice rumbled. "Do you understand me, soldier?"

Gordon's voice wavered. "Yes, perfectly, sir."

"Good. Any sign of Birchwood? He dropped off the grid a few months after his psych discharge."

"None, sir. He's kept a very low profile. There's got to be something to draw him out."

"He can't interfere with our acquisition of this child."

"I understand, sir."

"I tried to find a place for him after the accident. He's served this country well. But he's gone rogue. There's no controlling him."

"I'll make sure he doesn't compromise this mission."

"Report back in twenty four hours."

"Yes, sir."

General Holbrooke dropped the phone's handset back into its cradle.

There was one more loose end. A minor one, he hoped. Blake Farnsworth was still out there.

Up until now, the trust fund playboy grandson of Jack Farnsworth had wanted nothing to do with his grandfather's firm. The company had not wanted him, either. He had had no skills useful to F&G, unless they had wanted to stage a Broadway musical.

The only thing that had kept Blake and F&G chained together was the iron-clad trust fund agreement -- a set of golden handcuffs forcing the company to employ the playboy in some capacity.

The federal raid on the company's headquarters last year had put it out of business, freeing Blake from that employment obligation and releasing all the trust fund assets directly to him. Now that he had full control of his substantial trust fund, there was nothing keeping him tied down in Rapid City. The General had expected him to vanish into the celebrity strewn nightlife of New York or Los Angeles.

Instead, young Farnsworth had made an oversized donation to the city's hospital -- to fund a state of the art pathology lab in the hospital's newest wing.

The boy never had any interest in science or medicine, and no one believed that Farnsworth was actually interested in bettering the hospital. Twittersphere speculation was that he was trying to impress a woman.

Holbrooke didn't buy that explanation either. Farnsworth didn't have a philanthropic bone in his body and ran through women, and men, like a sailor on shore leave. Holbrooke believed there was a more devious reason for Farnsworth still living in the small city where his grandfather's company used to be. And where one of the four surrogates was about to give birth.

Holbrooke rubbed his scalp. He was missing something about Farnsworth but couldn't quite put his finger on it. He retrieved his unlit cigar stub, clamped it between his teeth, and returned to gazing at the wall of towering pine trees that obstructed his view of the horizon.

SUNDAY,
9:14 AM MDT

Doctor Leslie Stafford leaned over her patient, placed the silver disc of her stethoscope against the distended abdomen, and listened. The fetus's heartbeat resonated in her ears.

My god, this baby's strong. It's only thirty-six weeks but it sounds like forty-two. It's amazing how healthy it is despite all the problems that Julie has experienced during the pregnancy.

After a few moments she straightened and removed the stethoscope from her ears. She looked at her patient and smiled. "Sounds good. Are you ready for this?"

"As ready as I'll ever be," Julie replied. "The baby certainly is ready." She rubbed her belly, which seemed doubly enormous given her otherwise slight frame. "I am a little nervous about delivering this early."

Stafford place two fingers on Julie's thin wrist and eyed her watch. "Delivery at thirty-six weeks is not that unusual. Every baby is different. This one seems to be in good health, strong heartbeat, good size and birth weight. I'm not anticipating any problems. You're having contractions and you're dilating. Your body is saying it's time."

Julie nodded. "I know I should listen to my body, but I went full term for the last three. I guess I'm just nervous."

Stafford walked around Julie's bed and looked at the fetal monitor display. Everything was normal. "You've had a rougher than normal pregnancy. I'm actually a little relieved that you're delivering now and not four weeks from now. This pregnancy has seemed to drain you a lot more than the other three. Plus, I'll be glad to get you back in good health. It's almost like the baby knows that your body cannot take anymore and it's cutting you a break."

"I really appreciate you scheduling my delivery for the weekend, especially sending the car for me," Julie said. "I know it's not what you usually do."

"After the way you sounded on the phone yesterday, there was no way I was letting you take a taxi." Stafford smiled and winked. "You are one of my favorite patients, you know. A bit of a celebrity too, in a way. At least in the IVF circle. You've been a surrogate three times before for some rather noteworthy couples. I did have some misgivings about this one, though. They weren't a couple that I had screened for you, like the other three."

"They seemed like a nice couple, and they paid me well," Julie said. "More than usual. I don't know why they disappeared."

"We may never know," Stafford replied. "But we'll find this baby a good home."

"I'd never thought my life would end up like this. It's kinda weird. Sometimes, I feel like a prostitute, selling my body. But this is for a good cause, right? I'm helping to bring new lives into the world. Lives that will be cherished and nurtured."

"You're doing a beautiful thing, Julie."

"I remember the first time I did this. How I became a surrogate in the first place." Julie took Stafford's hand and looked her in the eyes. "You saved my life, Doctor. You helped me turn a hateful act into something meaningful and positive."

"You saved your own life, Julie. It was your idea."

"I thought my life was over after…." Julie closed her eyes for a moment. "… after it happened." Julie squeezed Stafford's hand. "Then I met you. It was like God was giving me a second chance. The most awful experience that I ever had became one of the most special, the most meaningful. It gave me a real purpose in life."

"Julie, it takes a very special person to make something so horrific into something positive. I'm proud of you."

Julie turned away and became quiet.

Stafford touched Julie's shoulder. "What's wrong?"

"If you're so proud of me, then why do you want me to stop? You led me here, now you want to take it away?"

"I don't want to take anything away from you, Julie, but your body can't do this anymore. I'm concerned about your health."

Julie closed her eyes and began to breathe rhythmically. "Another contraction?" Stafford asked.

Julie nodded her head and continued her steady breathing. She breathed one last cleansing breathe and then opened her eyes. "It's passed."

Stafford glanced at her watch. "Three minutes apart," she said.

"Doctor," Julie began. She hesitated for a moment. "I know we've talked about it before, but I am planning to do this again. To be a surrogate again."

Stafford placed her tablet on the table next to Julie's bed. She rolled a stool over to the bedside and took a seat. "Julie, this is your fourth pregnancy. You're getting older. Your body isn't what it used to be. Plus, you've had more than your share of complications this time."

"But plenty of women have more than four children. Some have six or seven or more. They show up on the news."

"Just because they had that many children, doesn't mean your body can."

"But Doctor, this is my livelihood. It's how I survive. What will I do? How will I live if I stop being a surrogate? Who will I be?"

"Julie, I understand that it will be a big transition, but you can do it. You've learned a lot about surrogacy these past few years. You could become a counselor. You could work at my IVF clinic, counseling other surrogate mothers. It's a starting point."

"It's not the same."

"You need to think of your body, Julie. You also need to think about the babies that you might carry if you continue being a surrogate. How would you feel if you lost a baby? It would be devastating, not only to you, but for the couple who entrusted the care of their unborn child to you. Could you live with that? I know that I couldn't. Also, I would be doing you a disservice as your doctor, and as your friend, if I encourage you to keep doing this."

Julie looked away.

Stafford stood. "I know I can't stop you, Julie. You can find another doctor. One who doesn't care about you, as a person. One who sees you only as a source of income. But the fact remains. Your body can't do this anymore."

Stafford's smartphone buzzed. She reached for it and swiped at the screen. "Julie, I need to handle this. You may be my favorite patient, but you're not the only one." She smiled. "You're in good hands with these two nurses. They're the best."

Nurse Melanie Connor came over to Julie's bed and placed a hand on Julie's arm. "You're going to be just fine, child. Me and Nurse Harlow are going to take good care of you." Her warm southern drawl lent an additional air of comfort to her words.

"Everything's looking good, Julie," Stafford said. "It won't be long now before you bring another beautiful child into this world." She squeezed Julie's hand, then turned and left the room.

Despite her assurances to Julie, Stafford felt uneasy -- that this delivery would be different. She couldn't put her finger on it. It was a gut feeling.

Julie's second and third trimesters were tougher than normal. She had experienced a number of symptoms and complications, including vitamin deficiencies, tiredness, irritability, malaise, weight loss, electrolyte imbalances, and dehydration.

One or two of these symptoms during a pregnancy would not be a major concern. Each was manageable. However, Julie had experienced a wide range of overlapping symptoms. The symptoms would appear and disappear as Stafford fought to keep them under control. Stafford would treat one, then another would appear. Subsequent ones would be brought under control, then earlier symptoms would return. Stafford had not seen such a spectrum of symptoms before in any of her patients.

At the nurse's station, Stafford scrolled across the screen of her smartphone, reviewing the message that had pulled her away from Julie. A new patient was scheduled to deliver next week, but her water had broken and she was on her way to the hospital.

With Julie, two other unscheduled deliveries, and now this new patient, the maternity ward had four deliveries. Deliveries were typically scheduled during the week when the hospital was fully staffed.

Julie's delivery was a special case. Stafford had planned Julie's delivery for this week-end, when other births were not typically taking place, so that she could focus on this one delivery. She had even called in a couple of favors so that her two best nurses would be on shift for the delivery. Now she would have to juggle four deliveries over the next twenty four hours.

Stafford checked the roster to see which other doctors were available; who was in; who was on-call. It was her and Doctor Rossini. Doctor Jackson was on-call. None of the mid-wives were available. Three doctors, four deliveries. A bit of juggling, but they should all be okay.

Stafford spoke to one of the nurses. "Please call Doctor Jackson. Tell him there are four deliveries and we need him here, stat."

"Yes, Doctor," the nurse replied.

Stafford returned to Julie's room, checked her vitals and spoke with the nurses.

"She had another contraction," Nurse Connor reported. "Stronger this time."

Stafford gave them a few more instructions. One of them wheeled a cardiac monitor over to Julie's bedside and untangled a set of multi-colored wires connected to the front panel.

"What's going on?" Julie asked. She looked at the nurse then to Stafford who was busy checking Julie's pulse.

"Your heart rate is a little elevated, but your blood pressure is low. We need to monitor them."

"Is there something wrong?"

"No, Julie. It's a precaution, that's all. Relax. I'm going to take very good care of you. Nurse Connor is going to place an automated blood pressure cuff on your left arm. You'll feel it pump up automatically every few minutes as it checks your blood pressure."

"What about all these wires on my chest?"

"Those are to monitor your heart rate."

"Is that necessary?" Julie tried to sit up. "You're scaring me, Doctor."

Stafford placed a hand on Julie's shoulder. "I'm going to take good care of you, Julie. I promise."

Julie settled back onto the pillows. "You're always looking out for me, Doctor. I appreciate it."

Stafford gave her a reassuring smile.

"I've never started delivery before my water broke. Isn't that weird?" Julie asked.

"It sometimes happens, Julie. It wouldn't be the first time for me to have to break a woman's amniotic sac while she was in labor. Just think, you won't have to clean-up the mess like the last three times," Stafford chuckled.

Julie huffed and puffed.

"Another contraction?" Stafford asked.

Julie squinted, gritted her teeth, then nodded her head. She breathed slowly and forcefully through her gritted teeth. Slowly the grimace left her face.

"Forty five seconds, Doctor," one of the nurses announced.

"Thank you. Julie, your contractions are still about three minutes apart. You don't seem to be progressing. I'll need to examine you again to check your effacement and dilation, okay?"

Julie took a breath. "Yes, Doctor. This baby wants out, I think."

One of the nurses pushed a pair of latex gloves onto Stafford's freshly scrubbed hands. With her foot, she guided a wheeled stool over to the foot of Julie's bed, took a seat, and lifted the sheet draped over Julie's legs. She peered around Julie's leg. "You okay?" Julie nodded and closed her eyes.

After a few moments passed, Stafford replaced the sheet over Julie's legs and rolled away from the bed. She stood and pulled off her gloves, tossing them into the nearby biohazard bin. "You're one hundred percent effaced," Stafford announced. "And fully dilated. Your contractions should be progressing."

"And my water hasn't broken yet."

"It looks like I'm going to have to do that." Stafford turned to Nurse Connor. "Could you prep please?" She turned back to her patient, who was fiddling with the edge of the sheet covering her. "Julie. I'm going to step out for a quick minute while the nurses prep you. Then I'll come back and we'll break your water and delivery this baby, okay?"

Julie began to speak. "Okay, doct…." Then her eyes clamped shut. Her legs tightened and her head lurched forward a bit. She sucked in air through her nose, then blew it out through clenched teeth.

"Another contraction," Nurse Connor said. "They're getting closer together now."

Stafford's phone buzzed again.

Damn.

She swiped its screen.

She's here already?

She looked at Julie, who was taking one final deep breathe. The contraction must have stopped. "Julie, I really need to step out for a minute. The nurses are going to prep you so that I can break your water. I'll be gone just a second. Okay?"

Julie nodded. "Please, Doctor, be quick."

She squeezed Julie's hand. "I'll be right back."

Stafford hurried out of the room and toward the nurse's station. When she reached the station counter, she asked, "Where's Doctor Rossini?"

"He's in delivery," the nurse behind the counter said.

"Where's Doctor Jackson? He's on call. You did page him?"

"Yes, he said he's on the way."

"He should be here by now. He practically lives next door. I've got a patient in active labor. I need Jackson to cover for this other incoming patient."

The nurse picked up her phone. "I'll call him again."

A scream rolled down the hallway. Stafford turned in time to see Nurse Harlow appear in the doorway of Julie's room. Her eyes were wide.

Stafford did not need another prompt. She ran toward the room. "What's the status?" she demanded as she entered. She looked at the floor at the foot of Julie's bed. A pool of blood-stained liquid was spreading over the polished tile.

"I'm not sure," Nurse Connor replied, her sunny southern accenting falsely sugarcoating the seriousness of her words. "We were prepping like you asked. She started having another contraction, …."

As if on cue another scream erupted from Julie's contorted face.

Doctor Stafford's eyes scanned across the array of monitors clustered at the head of the bed. Displays flashed red and yellow and the alarms merged into single pulsing wall of sound that screamed for attention. "Turn those damn alarms off!" Stafford demanded. She extended her arms and the second nurse shoved a pair of sterile gloves onto her hands.

Stafford leaned in toward her patient. "Julie! Breathe."

Stafford lurched back as Julie's contorted face flung itself forward, her gaping mouth emitting another ragged scream.

Julie clutched the edges of the birthing table, her fingernails digging deep into the soft padding. Her hospital gown barely covered her taut thighs as her legs strained against the stirrups.

Stafford spoke slowly and clearly. "Breathe."

Julie's teeth were clenched and her eyes shut tight.

"Breathe," Stafford urged.

"Julie!"

"Julie! Breathe! Take a breath. Let it out."

Julie's body slowly unwound and laid itself back onto the birthing table.

"That's good, Julie," Stafford coached. "Breathe. Focus on the breathing." She glanced over at the monitor screens. The heart rate displayed on the cardiac monitor was dangerously elevated."

"She's vomiting!" One of the nurses shouted.

Stafford turned back to see thick liquid oozing from Julie's lips and flowing down her chin. "Clear her airway!" she barked, then leaned in toward her gagging patient. "Julie. We need to help you breathe. I'm going to put a tube in your throat to help you breathe."

Nurse Connor repositioned Julie's head, held open her mouth, cleared the sticky liquid from Julie's airway, and then assisted Stafford with intubation. Julie's teeth clamped down on the endotracheal tube that Stafford was attempting to insert into Julie's throat.

"I'm trying, but she's fighting us. I can't intubate!" Stafford said.

As Stafford retracted the endotracheal tube, Julie flung herself forward again. Stafford retreated in time to avoid a spray of vomit that stained Julie's sweat-soaked gown with a red-green gruel.

Stafford could see Julie's lips moving, trying to form a word. She leaned in toward Julie's ear. "Julie! Can you hear me? Julie! It's Doctor Stafford. We're trying to help you."

23

Julie's head whipped back and forth, and then flung itself into Stafford's face. Stafford staggered back and grabbed at her nose, then withdrew and inspected her gloved hand. No blood. She ripped off the contaminated gloves and extended her arms. The sound of snapping latex told her that the nurse had placed a new pair of sterile gloves on her hands.

She returned her attention to her patient. Julie lay there, flopped over like a rag doll, her head almost resting on the bulging belly that held a precious new life. Stafford hesitated for a moment, and then readjusted the motionless heap of sweat and skin back into a reclining position.

An eerie quiet descended upon the room; nurses staring; the hush broken only by the single beep of the cardiac monitor, followed by a steady, flat tone.

"She's in V-fib!" Nurse Connor shouted.

The room came alive with a flurry of shouts for bag, paddles, intubation, defibrillator.

"We're losing her! Let's move!"

"Paddles." A nurse smeared a colorless gel onto the defibrillator paddles. Stafford rubbed them together and then shouted, "Clear!" Julie's chest sprang off the table when the massive pulse of electricity surged through her body.

The monotone from the cardiac monitor changed to a hesitant beeping. "Sinus rhythm!" shouted one of the nurses.

Stafford leaned close. "Julie! Stay with us, Julie!" She flashed her penlight across Julie's eyes and breathed a sigh of relief, only to be answered by the return of the steady, flat tone.

"She's asystole!" Nurse Connor shouted.

Stafford grabbed the paddles again. "Clear!" she shouted.

Another surge drove Julie's chest into the paddles as if they were powerful magnets. There was no change in the incessantly steady tone.

"Clear!" Stafford shouted again.

Another pulse from the paddles lifted Julie's body off the table.

"…. Clear! …. Clear! …."

Nurse Connor touched Stafford's shoulder. She stopped and stared down at the lifeless body of the young, pregnant woman. Julie's face was frozen in a contorted grimace; eyes wide; mouth agape; dribbles of red-green liquid on her lips and cheeks.

"Doctor!"

Stafford turned. Nurse Harlow was pointing at Julie's distended abdomen. Small bulges appeared and disappeared beneath the stretched skin of her stomach.

"We can still save the baby!" Stafford commanded. "Prep for emergency C-section."

Stafford and the nurses broke into a well-choreographed dance. Sterile instruments appeared. Blood oozed from the midline longitudinal incision sliced vertically down Julie's abdomen. Gloved hands reached in and withdrew the infant. A greasy cheese colored coating matted down the fine, reddish lanugo.

"That's a lot of caseosa, even for thirty-six weeks." Nurse Connor remarked.

"It's not full term." Stafford replied. "Clamp and cut."

The infant's umbilical cord was tied off. Stafford handed the infant to Nurse Connor. "Perform an APGAR, please."

Stafford looked down at the bloody, sweat soaked body that was her patient. A low monotone droned away in the background. Stafford reached out and punched at a button with a bloody gloved finger. She closed her eyes and breathed in the silence.

"I'll close," she whispered and started prepping for the procedure, but then stopped. She noticed that the umbilical cord was thicker and considerably longer than a typical human cord. "Nurse. Assistance, please." Stafford followed the length of the cord, withdrew the placenta from within the womb and placed it into the waiting stainless steel pan held by the nurse. "Get this to pathology. I want a full work-up."

Stafford glanced around the room. It was littered with latex gloves and torn sterile wrappers. Bile and blood stained the floor. The infant was in apparently good health and had already been whisked away to the nursery. She returned her attention to the bloody slit in Julie's abdomen. Using a pair of hemostats, she selected a curved suture needle from the tray and threaded the suture through its eye. Around her the whispering nurses were collecting bloodstained instruments.

One by one each nurse drifted away until only Stafford remained, bent over Julie's body. Stafford's head bobbed slightly and her hand moved slowly, rhythmically, like a prayer ritual, as she stitched close the wound.

MONDAY, 6:00 AM MDT

"I need you back to finish the mission."

Captain Robert Gordon sat at the edge of his bed, half clad, staring at his smart phone. The familiar voice at the other end was one that he hoped never to hear again. He rubbed the overnight growth of beard on his chiseled chin, and then brought the phone back to his ear. "What are you talking about? There's nothing to finish. The mission was aborted after the raid on F&G headquarters."

Birchwood's frosty tone dropped another twenty degrees. "You're mistaken, soldier. The mission is still viable."

Captain Gordon tried to picture his former superior officer on the other end of the line. Colonel John Birchwood, probably standing, statue-straight, in an empty hotel room. Gordon could feel the Colonel's cold, piercing stare. He felt the urge to salute.

"The first surrogate has given birth," Birchwood said. "She died during the birthing process." He reported the news as if he was announcing the results of a military exercise.

Gordon's lean frame shot off the bed. He started to speak but caught himself. He glanced back at Mary. She was snuggled in their bed, holding a Kindle and wearing ear buds. Gordon didn't take any chances; he kept his voice low and headed to the far corner of the bedroom as he spoke. "Oh my god!" he whispered. "We killed her? What about the baby? Is there one?"

"Yes. It is alive."

"Where?"

"At the city hospital. I need you and Sullivan to recover it."

"What? Are you serious? How are we supposed to do that?"

"You need to continue with your false identities. You should be able to recover the infant as its parents."

Gordon balked. "We can't just waltz into the hospital and claim that we're the baby's real parents. We have no proof."

"You have the surrogate contract."

"That's not going to be enough. They'll probably want to do a paternity test. That's not going to go well."

There was a long pause before Birchwood replied. "Your team is going to have to come up with an alternate recovery plan."

"No, John. My *team* doesn't need to do anything."

"You will address me properly, soldier!"

28

Gordon felt as if the phone was going to freeze against his ear. He blinked and shook his head. "Huh?"

"You will address me properly; as Colonel or sir."

Gordon closed his eyes and took a breath. "Fine, Colonel. Sir, there is nothing to be done at this point."

"Are you refusing to follow orders, soldier?"

Gordon took a leap. "John, I mean Colonel, sir. There is no mission. You're no longer in the military. Don't you remember? You were discharged after the incident."

The gruff voice at the other end shot back. "What are you talking about?"

"The explosion, sir. The destruction of the desert research facility. Don't you remember, sir?"

There was no response. Gordon could hear sharp, staccato breaths at the other end. He waited for a moment until the breaths became softer and more regular. "You didn't evacuate with the rest of the men," Gordon said, hoping to pull the Colonel back to reality. "They found you unconscious in what was left of your office. It was amazing that you survived. You were lucky that your office was located so far from the labs."

A couple of quick, sharp breaths filled Gordon's ear, then a voice said, "We still need to complete the mission."

"No, sir, we don't. The mission has been scrubbed, sir." Gordon paused, and then took a chance. "And it sounds like you're not fully recovered from the accident, sir. Are you attending your therapy sessions?"

Birchwood's voice regained its icy solidity. "Those sessions were a waste of time. They interfered with completion of the mission."

Gordon toed that fine line between advice and impertinence. "Those sessions are your only way to heal, Colonel. You've experienced a lot of mental trauma, sir. All your previous covert missions. The death of your younger brother. Now this. It's taken quite a toll on you, sir. I recommend that you stand down and let other capable officers complete the mission in their own way."

Icicles shot through the phone's speaker. "You can't dismiss me. I outrank you, Captain."

Gordon spoke softly and slowly. "Sir, I'm not dismissing you. I'm respectfully reminding you of the facts at hand. The scope of the mission has changed. Other operatives are taking over. I know it's difficult to be out of the loop, now, sir, but it's simply a fact. Your superiors, our superiors, have altered the mission parameters. A new set of operatives with skills appropriate to those new parameters have been deployed. We no longer have need-to-know for this mission."

Birchwood's voice barked back. "I'm in charge of this mission. I give the orders."

Gordon tried again to nudge Birchwood back toward reality. "Sir, General Holbrooke relieved you of this mission. Don't you remember? You received a medical discharge."

"Captain Gordon, you are refusing to obey the orders of your commanding officer. You are close to insubordination. I'm relieving you of your duties and I am placing you on disciplinary leave. I'll find a more competent officer to complete this mission."

Realizing the futility of the situation, Gordon replied, "Yes, sir. Thank you, sir." He nearly saluted, but caught himself. The line went dead. Gordon stood staring at his phone's blinking screen. His mind raced.

He's in worse shape than I thought. I've got Mary to deal with. Now I have a crazy colonel, too.

A voice from across the bedroom snapped him from his thoughts.

"Bob, honey. Was that who I think it was?"

Bob looked up. Lieutenant Mary Sullivan was propped up on an army of pillows against the headboard of their bed. Her golden blonde hair flowed down the creamy skin of her breasts, covering their areolas.

Focus, damn it! I spoke to Holbrooke only two days ago, right after we found Julie living in Rapid City. How the hell did Birchwood get that intel?

"Bob? Was that Colonel Birchwood?"

She reads my mind now?

Bob snapped himself back from the muddle of conflicting thoughts racing through his head.

Say something to her, you idiot.

"Um, yes. It was him." The words left his mouth as if someone else was speaking.

Mary looked like she was expecting the call. "What happened? What did he want?"

He placed the phone on his nightstand and slipped between the sheets.

Think fast.

"Um, he's trying to resurrect the mission."

"What mission? You mean the surrogate project?"

"Yes."

"You told me that mission was scrubbed."

Damn! Make up something to tell her.

"Birchwood has this crazy idea that the mission is ongoing. He says they impregnated Julie with a 'Thal zygote. He told me she carried to term but then she died during childbirth."

Mary bolted upright. Her breasts spilled out from behind their golden curtains. "Oh my god! Julie's dead? What happened? Where's the baby?"

Bob's mind was a jumble of conflicting thoughts and images. "Um, yes. There's a baby," he stammered. His mouth continued moving but he couldn't keep his eyes off Mary's hourglass figure.

Her eyes followed his. She yanked the sheets up to her shoulders with one hand. "Oh my god, Bob! Birchwood was just on the phone and all you can focus on are my breasts? Where's the baby? Is it alive?"

Gordon shook his head to clear his thoughts. "Yes, at the city hospital. I don't know any more than that."

Mary's lips formed the letter 'O'. Her free hand shot up to cover her mouth. Her eyes widened. She clutched the sheet tighter against her chest. "Do you think it's a real ....?"

"Possibly. I don't know. That genetics stuff was beyond me. I have no idea if it really worked. Or even if Birchwood's telling the truth."

"What if he is? What if there's a baby at the hospital that has no parents, no family, and is in danger of being abducted by a delusional Colonel who should be in a psych ward?" Mary's hand grabbed Bob's forearm. She locked eyes with her lover. "We need to rescue it," she said. "That baby's our responsibility."

Bob started to pull away, but caught himself. "Wait, what? How is it our responsibility?"

"Julie became pregnant because of us. She had that child because of us. Now she's dead…because of us."

Bob stared at Mary's wide, imploring eyes.

I need to tell her something. Anything to keep her from getting any more involved in this situation and to keep her sidelined while Walker and I rescue the baby.

"What can we do? It was a highly classified mission. We can't just go the hospital and tell them everything. They won't believe us. And even if they do, do you think that they would hand over that infant to us?

Mary's eyes narrowed. "This isn't a mission anymore. This is a baby's life we're talking about. They need to be told something. If the baby really is a Neanderthal, it's going to die."

Bob blinked. "Why do you say that?"

"I did some research after the mission was aborted. I wanted to find out if what they were trying to do was really possible," Mary explained. "It turns out that it wasn't as farfetched an idea as I had originally thought. But I figured that with the mission scrubbed at that point, Julie wasn't in any danger." Mary closed her eyes and shook her head. "I just assumed that Julie would think we found another surrogate and that she would move on with her life."

"I didn't realize how emotionally attached you were to Julie."

"How could I not be?" Mary shot back. "You know I had reservations about being involved in the mission. Yes, I volunteered. Because I knew you were going to be part of it." She looked down, but kept talking. "I didn't think through the consequences. I kept rationalizing away the deception that we were committing." She pressed the palm of her hand against her forehead. "Damn it!"

Bob put his hands on her shoulders and whispered. "I know it hurts. Julie's death is on both of us. But her baby is alive. The doctors at the hospital will take good care of it and find it a good home."

"You don't know that. It may not live."

"You keep saying that. You said that you did some research. Is there something that you learned about 'Thal babies?'"

Mary looked up at her lover. She brushed her flaxen hair away from her face and rubbed her eyes. "I read that the dietary needs of a Neanderthal may be different than humans. The doctors at the hospital won't know what to do."

Bob moved closer. "Mary. Sweetheart. We don't even know if it's a 'Thal. Maybe the cloning didn't work-out. Maybe this is a normal human baby," he said.

"And what if it's not? What if it's really a Neanderthal? A Neanderthal baby who's in danger of being kidnapped or dying from malnutrition? We can help them make the right decisions to keep it safe and healthy," Mary said.

Bob backed away. "What? You're going to waltz into a hospital, tell them they have a 'Thal in their maternity ward, that they need to feed it a special diet, and oh, by the way, there's a mentally unstable colonel who's going to try to kidnap it?"

"There must be something we can do?" Mary pulled the sheets tighter around her chest and bit her lower lip. Her green eyes appeared to search his face for a solution. "What if we adopt it?"

Where the hell did that come from?

"Adopt a baby? Mary, we're not even married. We can't adopt a baby."

"We could get married. You do love me, don't you?"

Bob held his breath for a moment.

Shit! This hole I'm digging just gets deeper and deeper.

He searched his partner's face for the right words to say.

"Mary, sweetie, I understand your concern about this child, but what would we do? If *we* take it, what are we going to do with it? What if it really is a 'Thal? We can't raise it. We don't know the first thing about raising a 'Thal. We'll probably end up killing it ourselves because we won't know what we're doing." He placed a finger under her chin. "Do you want that?"

"I don't know what I want. I only know that a young woman who trusted us is dead, and her baby is lying in a hospital. We owe her something,"

"We could contact the hospital. Anonymously. Give them enough info, just enough, so that they can save the baby's life and keep it safe," Bob said.

Mary abandoned the pillows and pulled herself into a kneeling position, dragging the sheets along with her. "We can start by contacting Julie's doctor. I'm sure we can find him," she said.

"And what would we tell him?" Bob asked.

"Enough to keep the baby alive and healthy. We may not be able to save this baby's life, but maybe the doctors can do it," Mary said. "They need to have the right dietary information."

Bob shook his head. "I don't think the doctors would take us seriously."

"Well, they won't be able to do anything if Birchwood steals it. And, we have no idea what he plans to do with it after. I don't think he's going to try to raise it." Mary glanced away. "Maybe he's going to kill it."

Bob laid a hand on hers. She turned back to face him. He stared into her bright, green eyes. "No. That's not going to happen. Birchwood sees this baby as a military asset. He wouldn't destroy it. He may try selling it to a military contractor who can continue the research. It's even possible that he might offer it to a country whose politics align more closely with his own."

"He wouldn't do that. He's too patriotic. He loves this country. He would never commit any act against it."

Bob shook his head. "This is not the Birchwood you remember. I know him better than you. Longer. I know his past. The man's gone off the deep end. He's not thinking straight. He may have convinced himself that his country's turned against him. He's so fixated with what happened to his brother in Afghanistan, he could do anything."

Mary squeezed Bob's hand. "We need to do something. Before the baby gets hurt or dies."

Bob closed his eyes and drew a breath.

Damn it! This isn't going to work. How am I supposed to finish this mission with Lieutenant Walker and keep Mary on the sidelines?

"Bob?"

She's infatuated by this baby. She's becoming as obsessed as Birchwood.

"Honey?"

Why the hell did Birchwood call me here? Wait! How did he even get this number? Shit! I bet he knew that Mary would be here, too.

"Bob, honey? What are you thinking?"

This whole mission is unraveling fast. Forget Walker. I'm going to have to do this with Mary. Holbrooke's going to have my hide, but there's no other choice. I'm going to have to make it work.

"Bob!"

Gordon snapped back. "Okay. We can go to the hospital. Tomorrow, not today. I need to contact Holbrooke first. We have to be careful about how we do this. They can't learn who we really are, or about the mission or any connection to the military. They're going to eventually figure out that this baby is not human. The sicker it gets, the more tests they're going to run. It's going to come out eventually. Then the baby's diet will be adjusted. However, we can't have any trail leading back to us or the military; otherwise this is going to completely blow up in our faces. We have to do this in a way that is plausible."

"How are we going to do that?"

"We return to the original mission profile."

Mary's eyes lit up. "You mean, pretend that we're adopting the baby?"

Gordon forced the words out of his mouth. "We need to reestablish our cover story about being surrogate parents. But only to rescue the child from Birchwood. That's it."

Mary threw her arms around him. "Oh, Bob. I love you!" She planted a sloppy kiss on his face.

Gordon's mind seized up. The right side of his brain tried to move his arms to release himself from Mary's grip. The left side kept his lips pressed against hers. The right side won. Barely. He wiped his face with the back of his hand and took Mary by the shoulders. "Wait, Mary. We're not really adopting this child. You know that, don't you?"

She smiled back and ran her fingers through his hair. "Of course, honey. Why would I think anything else?"

Gordon clamped his eyes shut. His head drooped forward.

Fucking Holbrooke. Why does he always have to be right about everything!

MONDAY,
9:01 AM MDT

Captain Robert Gordon paced a tight circle in the cramped office that he shared with Lieutenant Mary Sullivan. He had managed to requisition some space in the basement of the Federal Courthouse. It wasn't much, but it gave him access to the secure phone line that he needed to communicate with the General.

He reached for the phone's handset, then stopped.

It's like ripping off a bandage. Just got to do it.

He picked up the handset, punched in the long series of security codes on the keypad, then waited for the connection to complete. He held his breath. After a few moments he heard the General's phlegm laden voice in his ear. "Holbrooke."

"Captain Robert Gordon reporting, sir."

He heard the general clearing his throat, then ask, "Status?"

"Birchwood's on the move, sir."

"What's that?"

"He contacted me early this morning. He was trying to recruit the Lieutenant and me to retrieve the baby."

"You need to stop him. You can't let him get to that child. Does he know where Julie is?"

"Unfortunately, yes." Gordon paused. "There's another complication, sir. Julie has already given birth."

"What? Already? I'm no expert but this seems a few weeks early."

"It gets worse, sir. Julie is dead."

"Dead? How? Don't tell me that Birchwood killed her to get the child."

"No, nothing like that. From what Birchwood told me, she died during childbirth."

"Birchwood told you this? How the hell does he know what happened to Julie? Don't tell me that he has the child."

"He doesn't have the child. That's why he contacted me and the Lieutenant. He must have been doing some recon to determine how to extract the infant from the maternity ward. That's probably how he learned about Julie's death."

"You need to find him. And stop him. He can't get that child before we do. There's no telling what he'll do with it. I can't imagine the cluster-fuck if this gets out to the press. Or worse, to those jackass comedian newscasters on late night TV."

"There is one more problem, sir."

"Now what. Don't tell me it's about Lieutenant Sullivan."

"It's about Lieutenant Sullivan, sir."

"Christ, Gordon. I warned you about her. Hell, I warned you about yourself. That girl screws with a guy's head. I don't know how she made it this far in this man's army. She was never officer material. I blame it on all this PC bullshit. No one wants to come right out and say it and they ain't got the balls to discharge her." A long, slow throat-clearing filled Gordon's ear before Holbrooke's raspy voice asked, "What kind of crap did she pull now?"

"She wants to adopt the baby."

"What baby? You mean Julie's baby? Is she out of her fucking mind? She does realize it's a fucking experiment, doesn't she?"

"I tried to explain it to her."

"Well, explain it again."

"She feels responsible for Julie's death."

"How does she know Julie's dead? Did she talk with Birchwood?"

"Uh, no sir. Not directly. She was in the room when I took his call."

"She was in the office with you that early in the morning?"

"Um, no, sir."

"Don't say it soldier."

"She was in bed with me."

"Damn it, Gordon. I told you to stay away from her. She's like a siren. Worse. She wiggles her way under your skin like a sad-eyed basset hound. Before you know it, you're giving her foot massages and driving her to hair appointments. You need to get her under control and then out of your life."

"I will, sir."

"She's not assisting you and Lieutenant Walker with the extraction, is she?"

"Um, no sir."

"That's the correct answer, soldier. Stick to the alternate mission profile. You and Walker get to that hospital, find Julie's doctor, find that baby, and find a way to get it out of there without a fuss. Posing as a gay couple who want to be adoptive parents will work. Damn, you should have done it that way for the original surrogate meeting with Julie. You wouldn't have this mess with Lieutenant Sullivan."

The line went dead. Gordon looked at the handset, and then set it back into its cradle.

Walker.

A shiver went down Gordon's spine. It wasn't that he was homophobic or anything, but … he'd rather finish this mission with Mary. There was something about her that attracted him. He couldn't put his finger on it. It was true, she was a handful. And when he analyzed it logically, she was not someone he'd want to have a long term relationship with. She was emotional and unpredictable. But yet, there was something intoxicating about her personality. A man couldn't help but want to be entangled with her.

He thought again about the General's recommendation to work with Walker. Gordon shook his head.

Mary will work out fine. We're both military officers. Worst case, I'll pull rank on her.

MONDAY,
1:22 PM MDT

Colonel John Birchwood inspected the rows and columns of identical cribs neatly aligned behind the plate glass that enclosed the nursery. Each cradled a new life; a potential soldier, mathematician, scientist. Despite their obvious differences in complexion and facial features, all these infants were essentially identical. Practically clones of each other.

Except for one. Second row, fourth from the left.

A living, breathing 'Thal. The first in a new line of super soldiers.

Swaddled in a white blanket with wide pastel pink stripes, that infant lay sleeping. Tufts of fire-red hair peeked out from beneath the brim of a light pink knit cap. Its features hinted of both Asia and the Caucasus. It was an eclectic mix of wide, flat nose, large round eyes, prominent forehead, and peach-white skin. Its potential was unknown.

Birchwood pulled a crumpled photo from his breast pocket. The last photo of his youngest brother, Marcus, with his squad; dressed in camos; rifles in hand; fat grins on their faces. Taken only a few days before Marcus was blown to bits; his dismembered body strewn along a dirt road.

Birchwood bowed his head. His lips moved as if in prayer.

This is for you, Marcus. For your wife, your children. For all the troops who've lost their lives, needlessly. No longer will our men be slaughtered by fanatics with IEDs, or extremists who blow themselves up for some archaic world view.

He caught a glimpse of his reflection in the polished glass wall separating him from the dimly lit nursery.

History will vindicate me. Families of those troops whose lives we've spared will thank me.

The face of the uniformed officer in that reflection was of his brother.

Together, you and I will make history.

Birchwood placed the crumpled photo back into his pocket, spun on his heel and returned to his post. The maternity ward nurses mostly ignored him as he stood sentry in the hallway opposite the expanse of glass separating him from the child. He appeared and disappeared at seemingly random intervals as he patrolled the nursery; looking for weaknesses; chinks in the armor, cracks in the fortress.

Birchwood had not been in a civilian hospital for many years, and never in a maternity ward. He hadn't realized the layers of security protocols that were in place. There was no way he, or anyone, was going to simply waltz out of here carrying a baby that didn't belong to them. Without Captain Gordon or

Lieutenant Sullivan assisting him, the task of extracting this child was going to be considerably more difficult, but not impossible. He had succeeded as a lone operative on far more complicated and more dangerous missions.

In his mind, he reviewed all the events and intel gathered over the past twenty four hours.

The hospital's policy for observation of a newborn prior to discharge was a minimum of forty-eight hours. That was to allow sufficient time to perform physical examinations and monitor for appropriate vital signs, feeding and other bodily functions.

For most fathers experiencing the miracle of childbirth, the pacing would be over at this point and they would be by their wife's side, or bragging to friends and relatives about their sons' or daughters' future as an athlete or celebrity. For Birchwood, the mental pacing had just begun.

Due to the death of the gestational surrogate, the infant was being bottle-fed. This in itself was an additional complication and an added risk that had to be dealt with. Although it was unlikely that the surrogate's own breast milk would properly nourish the baby, the standard hospital formula would certainly not have the proper balance of nutrients to keep the baby in good health. This was the first of the four cloned 'Thals to be born. There was no way to anticipate how it would react to an artificial human food source.

Birchwood remembered the project scientists telling him that there was a seventy two hour window before the infant's diet would need to be altered to achieve normal Neanderthal growth and development. The improper diet alone provided at least two possible scenarios. The first was that the feedings would be sufficient to keep the baby in good enough health to allow for normal discharge.

Birchwood thought this might be the optimal outcome, as it would get the baby out of the hospital without incident. He could then intercept it on the way to the foster care parent's home, or remove it from the home covertly.

However, if the baby's health did not improve, its stay in the nursery would be extended. More tests would be run; tests that might reveal the true nature of the child. This was the worst case scenario.

He had not anticipated this surrogate's death. It both simplified and complicated the matter. On one hand, there was one less soldier in the enemy's nest. It narrowed the possibilities and outcomes. On the other hand, there were fewer scenarios from which to choose a possible strategy. It gave him fewer options. He wasn't yet sure if this was an advantage or disadvantage. He needed more intel.

Unfortunately, all the project data had been destroyed along with the secret desert installation. This included all the medical data that was collected about the surrogate, her pregnancy, 'Thal physiology, and anything else that might be helpful.

Destruction of the installation was necessary; its location was compromised. The mere fact of its existence at all warranted its destruction. General Holbrooke's orders to Birchwood were to transfer all the data off-site prior to leveling the compound. For some reason that he couldn't recall, the transfer never occurred. All the information was lost.

Now Birchwood was forced to rely on his memory, and his head for science was not as sharp as it was for military strategy and tactics. For the first time, Birchwood wished he had Doctor Summerston with him. The scientist was a complete asshole, but he knew 'Thal physiology.

Birchwood sorted through his memories for scraps of project data. He needed ammunition that he could use to help formulate a strategy to extract the baby.

There were four candidate surrogates who had been impregnated. According to the contract, all surrogates were to be paid to carry the child to term, relinquish all parental rights, and have no further contact with the child. The surrogates knew nothing about the true nature of the infants they were carrying.

He knew the background checks done prior to meeting with this surrogate had indicated that she was an excellent candidate for the cloning project. She had the reputation of a surrogate for well-to-do clients who were too busy or too self-absorbed to burden themselves with the day-to-day trials and tribulations of a pregnancy. She had carried designer children to term before; this had been no different, except that the genetics of this infant were truly designed.

The Colonel dug deeper into his memories and remembered the briefing meetings. This surrogate was an only child; her parents had died in a car accident when she was young. She was raised by her maternal grandparents, who have since passed on. She had no other family and few real friends. It was this lack of connections that had pushed her to the top of the candidate list.

Her medical profile had indicated that she was in minimal risk of complications. Collateral damage was not expected. Of course, there were no guarantees, but the suddenness of her death after the modified gestational period was completely unexpected.

The cloning team had assured Birchwood and General Holbrooke that the pregnancies would progress without incident; that human and 'Thal physiology was close enough that complications were no more likely than with normal human pregnancies. They based their assessment on the paleo-forensic data they had discovered which indicated humans and 'Thals successfully interbred over 38,000 years ago. Birchwood was now calling that assessment into question.

Birchwood squeezed shut his eyes as he tried to block nearby voices intruding into his thoughts. A couple of excited grandparents stood a few feet away, waving and welcoming their grandchild into the world.

He turned away and took a few steps, then realized he was heading toward the nurses' station. He turned back and looked down the hall. The grandfather was making monkey faces at a crying infant while his wife attempted to soothe the newborn through the thick plate glass.

He looked back toward the nurse's station. He recognized the surrogate's physician, Doctor Leslie Stafford, standing at the station desk. She was swiping the screen of her tablet while speaking with one of the nurses. Birchwood slowly approached the desk, tuning out the grandparents' voices and all other ambient noise, until the only voices in his head were from Stafford and the nurse.

Birchwood stopped, closed his eyes and listened. He could hear that Stafford was concerned about a baby's health. The recent blood work was abnormal. Lab results indicated atypical electrolyte levels.

Birchwood strained his memory.

Electrolytes. Minerals. Dissolved in water.

His technical training was still serving him. He refocused his attention to the conversation. He continued to parse key words and phrases from the conversation.

"Additional workup required," he heard. "Possible gastrointestinal inflammation. Metabolic disorder. Placental dysfunction. Risk of seizure, brain damage, coma and death."

This was not good, Birchwood thought. At best, this would delay discharge of the baby. At worst, the baby would die and an autopsy would be performed. All intermediate scenarios led to additional testing, any of which could reveal the true nature of the infant.

He returned his focus to the conversation. Stafford was instructing the nurse on changes to the baby's diet. This information might help Birchwood determine his next move. He closed his eyes and focused on the conversation.

A child's screech broke his concentration.

Damn civilians.

A vital piece of information was not acquired.

Birchwood turned to look down toward the other end of the hallway. The grandparents had been replaced by a disheveled young man holding a crying toddler in one arm while his other arm was being yanked out of its socket by a small boy attempting to push the elevator call button on the opposite wall.

The man was pleading, "Jack! Come here. Don't you want to see your new sister? Jack!"

The toddler's squirming forced the father to let go of Jack, who immediately bolted through the narrow gap of the closing elevator doors.

The disheveled dad lurched toward the elevator as its doors slid shut on the youngster's mischievous grin. "Jack! No!" He pounded on the call button, then looked up at the rapidly increasing display of the elevator floor indicator. "Shit," he muttered, glanced around, then hustled toward the stairwell with the toddler clinging to his neck.

"Excuse me, sir," a woman's voice said from behind Birchwood. He turned to face a short, full-figured blonde woman dressed in green scrubs; a stark contrast to the elegant apparel she had worn when greeting the surrogate at the hospital entrance. The ID hanging on her lanyard read 'Dr. Stafford, Leslie'.

Birchwood immediately took control of the conversation. Feigning a pleasant southern accent, he said, "Good afternoon, Doctor Stafford. I'm Colonel John Birchwood. May I help you?"

The Colonel had been trained to read body language and saw that this unexpected, direct introduction had caught the doctor off-guard. The technique was designed to interrupt a person's train of thought.

He smiled and nodded toward her ID badge.

She looked down and then made that 'oh, of course' expression.

Birchwood maintained control of the conversation. "It's tragic," he said while watching her face for any signs of micro-expressions that might be revealing. "A young woman like Julie, in the prime of her life, taken from this world so suddenly after such a normal pregnancy."

"Oh, you knew Julie?" Stafford asked.

"Yes, yes I did. Her father and I served together. I remember how devastated Julie was when her parents were killed in that accident." Birchwood paused to see if Stafford reacted; to see if she knew about the accident. "I believe that's what drove her to help others bring new lives into this world." He shook his head, sighed, and then glanced toward the rows of cribs. "Now this."

"Yes. It is tragic." Stafford replied.

Southern charm and colloquial expressions might help to get her to trust me and share what information she knows.

"How is the baby doing?" he asked. "I do hope that the poor little thing is doing okay." He glanced up toward the ceiling, then lightly touched Stafford on the arm. "I know that Julie trusts you to take good care of the baby."

"She's doing well," Stafford said. "So far, everything's normal." Her eyes did not betray her response.

This is going to take a little extra effort. She's good, but not that good.

Birchwood kept questioning her. "Julie was such a healthy young lady. Always eating right. And exercising. It's so horrible that she died like this. And in such a well-equipped hospital." He leaned in a bit and whispered, "Do you know how it happened?"

"No," she lied. "We're waiting for the autopsy results. Hopefully they will reveal the cause of death."

There it was. Birchwood caught the 'tell'. The tiniest of muscle motions. A milliseconds-long twitch at the left corner of Stafford's mouth. Imperceptible to the untrained eye.

She's withholding something. Or she's suspicious.

Birchwood continued to lead the conversation.

"But the baby's doing well?" he asked.

Another micro-expression betrayed her.

"Yes, everything's normal," she responded.

"What a relief," he feigned. "That's wonderful. I'm sure that will help make the foster placement go a little more smoothly.

"We don't have any foster placement yet."

Of course you don't. You're lying to me. This baby's going to be here for observation and testing for at least a week. Possibly two.

"Well, perhaps I can help with that. You know that the military takes care of their own. I'm in touch with other military families. I know that some of them would consider it an honor to raise the child of a decorated veteran."

"Well. That's very nice, but I'm not the one you need to speak with. You'd have to contact the hospital administration."

A low tune played from Stafford's hip. She reached down for her smart phone and swiped the screen. "I apologize, but I must be going now. Please excuse me."

Birchwood watched as Stafford strode to the elevator. She punched the call button a few times. When the elevator doors slid open, she stepped in, spun on her heels and punched one of the buttons on the panel. As the doors slid closed, their eyes locked for a moment.

Damn! This girl's going to be a real pain in the ass. She better not get in the way of this extraction.

TUESDAY,
6:11 AM MDT

He's going to kill it. I know he is. That's the type of man he's become. I need to save that child, before, ... before it's too late.

A shudder went down Mary's spine. She didn't want to think about it, about how he could kill the child, but her thoughts had their own agenda.

Mary sat alone at her kitchen table, waiting for her meds to kick in. The events over the past twenty four hours had proved too stressful for her to handle. She hated using the pills; they made her brain foggy. But, her usual coping techniques weren't working. Besides, maybe a foggy brain wouldn't be so bad right now. Anything to take her mind away from the face she saw yesterday.

Her hyper-associative mental capabilities had been an asset all through her career. They gave her an edge when solving complex problems with many variables.

However, over the past year, she had begun losing the ability to control the multitude of paths and

53

possibilities generated by her hyper-active brain. Thoughts formed and rushed through her mind at will, triggered by the slightest sensory input, or the recollection of some other memory.

She was seeing a civilian doctor about it. So far, the medical tests hadn't revealed any brain tumors and all her blood work and other tests were normal. Mary hadn't told Bob and she avoided seeing a military doctor. A psychological or neurological problem would be a blemish on her medical record and jeopardize her career.

She stirred a cup of coffee and stared out the window as she tried to focus on anything but the fears that permeated her mind.

A hummingbird was hovering around the feeder that hung outside. It flitted and darted around the slender cylinder filled with nectar.

She watched the feeding bird and let her mind run free, hoping that this mundane activity would squash the unwanted thoughts.

Her analytical brain latched onto the minutest of details. The feeder had fake flower petals molded into its plastic body to make it look more like the real thing. Mary wondered if it made any difference. Did the hummingbird really care about the aesthetics of a bird feeder? She couldn't imagine that the plastic petals were representational of any actual living flower. It was simply a cheap plastic feeder.

Probably made in China by child labor.

The chances that someone actually did any research to assure that these painted plastic petals looked like a flower that was native to this part of North America was virtually zero.

As though it was reading her thoughts, the hummingbird suddenly flitted away.

Ha! You heard me, didn't you, she laughed to herself. *Go find some real flowers, they probably taste better anyway.*

She stopped stirring the coffee and took a sip. It was cold.

Jeez, how long have I been sitting here?

She shook her head at the thoughts that came flooding back into her mind. Thoughts that had haunted her all night, had her awake at the break of dawn, and forced her out of bed, leaving Bob alone, snoring soundly as if without a care.

How would he do it? Would he walk into the maternity ward like he did yesterday and shoot it point blank? No, how would he get a firearm into the hospital? They have metal detectors.

She thought about that.

Do they have metal detectors? Shit. Maybe not. I didn't see any when I was there yesterday.

Her mind raced.

Shit! He's going to walk in there, shoot the infant in the head, and walk out. He's a trained killer. No one's going to be able to stop him. Certainly not the rent-a-cop security that the hospital has.

She took a breath.

Okay Mary, get a hold of yourself. Nothing's happened yet. Maybe he's not going to kill it after all. He could have easily done it yesterday.

She breathed in and out, slowly, deliberately, like the therapist taught her. She could feel the thoughts in her head slowing down. She tried to reach for them. Gather them up. Put them in a box. They slipped through her fingers.

Maybe that was just his recon. Maybe he was checking out the hospital security and floor plan and now he's going to go back to complete the mission.

In her mind she kept scooping at the thoughts that swirled in her head.

But, now that I know he's there, I can stop him. He's not the only one who has training. I just need to figure out how to get the baby to safety. I can do this.

The gears in her head turned as she worked through possible scenarios. Her hand lifted the cup of coffee to her lips.

"You're up early."

Mary jumped, startled by Bob's voice behind her. Cold coffee splashed from her cup onto her face and spilled down the front of her sweatshirt.

"Ah. Damn it!"

She put down the cup and reached for the napkins sitting in the holder in the center of the table. She turned as she wiped the coffee off her face and dabbed at her wet shirt.

Bob stood there, dressed only in boxers, a sheepish grin on his face.

"Sorry. I didn't think I was that quiet coming down the stairs," he apologized. "You must have been deep in thought."

He leaned down and kissed the top of her head, then padded over to the Keurig that was on the kitchen counter.

"What were you thinking about, honey?" he asked her as he perused the selection of K-cups on the carousel next to the coffee maker. He spun it around a few times then held a finger out. The K-cups spun past his finger like a game show wheel of prizes.

Mary didn't answer. She wasn't sure how to start the conversation. She looked back out the window. The hummingbird had returned. Or maybe it was a different one.

The snap of a K-cup being loaded into the Keurig and the hiss of pressurized water pulled her attention back.

Bob turned away from the machine to face her.

"I know you're thinking about something," he said. "I know that face. I can see the wheels turning in your head," he smiled.

"It's about yesterday."

"Yesterday? You need to be a little more specific, honey."

"I saw him at the hospital."

Bob stared at her. "You went to the hospital?"

"I'm sorry. I had to see the baby."

Bob's right hand shot up to his forehead. "Jeez, Mary, Do you know how dangerous that is? Not only for the baby, but for you. We were supposed to go today. Together. What possessed you to go alone?"

"I had to see it. I went up to the maternity ward. I was stepping out of the elevator when I saw him."

"Who? Wait." His eyes grew wide. "Not Birchwood?"

"Yes."

Bob grabbed his forehead with both hands. "Christ, Mary. Did he see you?"

"No, his back was toward me, but I knew it was him. He was having a conversation with a doctor or nurse or someone, … I didn't recognize her."

The Keurig hissed a last puff of air, signaling that the coffee was brewed. Bob ignored it and came over to the table to sit across from her. "You heard the conversation I had with Birchwood yesterday morning. The man is dangerous. We have no idea what he's planning. Why didn't you tell me about this?"

Mary felt as if her brain was bogged down in mud. Emotions fought their way into her consciousness but were tamped down by some invisible force.

The meds are kicking in.

"I'm sorry. I wanted to. I did." Her voice sounded flat. She tried to add some emotions to the words that left her lips. "I didn't know how … how you would react."

"Are you certain that he didn't see you?" he asked.

"Yes. I ducked back into the elevator."

"Good." Bob rubbed the growth of beard on his face. He looked down, as if in thought. "This is going to move up the timeline," he mumbled.

"Timeline? What timeline? What are you talking about?" she asked.

Bob looked away. He ran his hand through his hair, then turned back to face her. After a moment he responded, "Um, I contacted General Holbrooke. He was the one who was running the entire 'Thal breeding project before it was cancelled."

The thought of another possible ally against Birchwood fired up her mind. "Is he going to help us adopt the baby?" she asked.

"He wants to have it placed in a home. With a military family to raise it. Sort of like a witness protection program."

They're going to make it live with strangers.

"Why can't we do that? Why can't we raise it ourselves?"

"Mary, come on. We're not married or even engaged. I know you want to have a family someday. I do, too. But this is too soon, don't you think?" He took her hands in his. "We'll have children together. Our own children. When we're both ready."

She pulled her hands away and shook her head as she fought to yank away the blanket of medication that covered both the fear and the anger that was building in her belly.

"Damn it, Bob. You know how I feel about this. We owe it to Julie to raise that child."

"We owe it to Julie to find a good home for the child, that's all," he countered. "We're not ready for a kid of our own."

Mary's fist came down hard on the tabletop. "I am to ready! Stop treating me like I'm some fragile flower."

"Whoa! Calm down. What are you angry about? I'm just stating the facts. It's not time for us to start a family, Mary. Think about it. We're moving around on military assignments. It's not the right time for a kid."

"Plenty of couples deal with unexpected pregnancies," she blurted. "They make it work."

Bob threw his hands upward. "Are you listening to yourself? You're not thinking clearly. And you keep obsessing about adopting this baby. This isn't an unexpected pregnancy. And even if it was, there would at least be nine months warning. A couple would have time to prepare. They aren't suddenly handed an infant one day out of the blue." He leaned toward her. "And they aren't handed a Neanderthal infant. They'd have a human child."

Mary expelled a puff of air through her nose, but said nothing.

Bob straightened in his chair. "Listen, honey. I promise to find a really good home for this child. A loving home. But it can't be us. It has to be someone equipped and trained to raise such a special kid. Remember, no one's ever done this before. I can't imagine us even getting authorization to adopt."

The two sat in silence for a moment, then Mary asked, "So what are we going to do?"

"I've started planning that out," Bob said as he rose from his chair to rescue the coffee cup he'd left in the Keurig. He fussed over the creamer and sweetener, keeping his back toward Mary as he spoke. "The first order of business is to get the child out of the hospital before Birchwood makes his move." He finished adding powders to his coffee mug and stirred. "I wish we knew more about his plan."

"I know where he's staying," Mary announced.

Bob turned quickly, nearly spilling the contents of his mug. "What?"

"I followed him back to his motel."

"You did what? Mary, you could have gotten yourself killed!" Bob returned to the table. "He knows what you look like. If he spotted you, …."

"He didn't see me. I waited for him to leave the hospital. Then I followed him." Mary crossed her arms. "You and Birchwood are not the only ones trained in how to tail a vehicle without getting spotted."

Bob raised a hand. "Training and actual field experience are two different things. You've never been a field operative before."

She glared back at him. "You don't think I have the skills?"

Bob shook his head. "It's not that. I don't want to lose you. You weren't even supposed to be assigned to the original surrogate parent meeting with Julie. It was me who got you placed on that mission. I wanted to see how we would have worked together. Remember, I had to pull a few strings to get you on it. I argued that your knowledge of adoption and surrogacy law would be an asset in the field. You were the one who wrote up all the surrogacy contracts that were going to be used. I had assured General Holbrooke that you would not get emotionally invested in the mission." He paused for a moment. "You do remember that, don't you?"

Mary nodded.

He's right. I am emotionally involved. But why shouldn't I be? It's my fault that this baby lost its mother.

"So what's our next move?" she asked.

"Probably the best move is to try to use the surrogacy contract to get possession of the child."

"Possession?' she asked. "You make it sound like it's a piece of property."

"You know that's not what I mean. I just don't know all the terms. That's why I had you as my partner for the original mission. You're the one with the legal training. What's it called? Guardianship?"

Mary managed to stay focused and on topic. "It varies. In this state it's considered an arranged adoption, even if the genetic material is from the donors, the intended parents, and not from the woman actually carrying the child."

"Is that going to complicate matters?"

Mary thought for a bit. "Yeah. Probably. An adoption like this requires that the birth mother surrender her parental rights, even though technically she's not the biological mother of the child, but a gestational surrogate."

"So, with Julie dead, this gets complicated."

"Yes, it does. In the eyes of the law, the legal parent is dead and this child is an orphan. We, or any other potential parents, would have to go through the normal adoption process. There's no guarantee that we would be awarded custody."

"Doesn't the surrogacy contract come into play? What was the point of that?"

"There was no intention of having Julie give birth in this state. The plan was to have her give birth within a military installation, where states' adoption laws don't apply. The contract is useless. It was never really meant to be valid in any state."

Bob scratched his head. "Can we do anything with it? It has to have some value."

"Well, we might be able to use it as leverage with the courts for the adoption placement. If we can argue that this was Julie's intent, for us to be the parents, then we might at least be put at the top of the list. Having Julie's doctor on our side would help too. If we could get him or her to back us up, to convince the judge that this is in the best interest of the child, then we have a real shot at it."

"In the meantime, we need a contingency plan," Bob said. "In case we can't pull off the adoption. I'll work on that. Plus we'll need to be ready in case

Birchwood makes his move." He looked at the ceiling and bit at his lower lip. "We'll need to find Julie's doctor, whoever he is." He turned back to Mary. "Are you up for another visit to the hospital tomorrow? This time in our surrogate parents role. You remember the identities we had?"

"Of course I do! James and Linda Williams." She winked. "How could I forget that day, pretending to be the suburban mom-to-be? I was born for that role."

TUESDAY,
8:32 AM MDT

Doctor Leslie Stafford rubbed her eyes, and then went back to scrolling through the patient's medical data on her laptop screen. Copies of medical records and lab reports were spread across her desk, surrounding the laptop like an encroaching army.

There's got to be something. Anything. Julie was a perfectly healthy surrogate mother. No hypertension. No diabetes. No Rh factor. Nothing.

She shuffled the reports, charts and printouts around the polished glass and steel desktop as if they were puzzle pieces, hoping that a pattern would reveal itself and all would fall into place. She leaned back into the chair, stretched out her arms and let out a sigh.

Stafford gazed around her office. She had replaced the standard issue, mass produced office furniture found in most of the other doctors' offices with custom designed Italian pieces that looked more like sculptures than desks, chairs, and tables. One office wall was adorned with photos of smiling parents cradling their precious newborns. The opposite wall held framed parchments full of Latin words written in undecipherable fonts. She looked down at the disaster on her desk then leaned back her head and closed her eyes.

There was a knock at her office door. She sat up. "Come in. It's open." She grabbed the Missoni crochet-knit scrunchie off the desk and pulled her long blonde hair into a ponytail.

Doctor Eric Patterson poked his head into the room. "Any luck?"

"Eric. Come in." Leslie stood and waved him into the room. She straightened the green hospital scrubs that concealed her plus-size hourglass figure and came around her desk. "I was afraid you were going to be one of the hospital attorneys."

"This definitely must be a serious case," Eric said. "It's not often I see you in scrubs in your office. You look like a wreck. You weren't here all night, were you?"

"I slept on the couch." She managed a smile, but it fell away as soon as she started speaking. "It's been a crazy couple of days." She walked toward him. "I really missed you, too." She ran her hands over the lapels of his tailored suit that draped his rugged physique. "I knew this would look good. It complements you. Much nicer than those off-the-rack suits you buy. And you trimmed your beard like I suggested. I bet the women at the conference were checking you out," she winked.

Patterson blushed. He pushed some loose strands of her silken hair back behind her ear. "I read your emails and texts. I wish I had been here for you instead of at that boring medical conference." He took her hand and turned as if to lead her away. "You need to get out of here. Get some breakfast and a hot shower."

She pulled him back, laid a hand on his chest, and slid it down and around to the small of his back. Their lips met and parted. She felt the squeeze of his strong hands as they followed the curve of her hips. Stafford melted into his muscular frame. "I know," she murmured, but then pushed away from him. She waved at the pile of papers on her desk. "I can't figure this out. I've had this patient for years. Never a problem. One of the healthiest women I've known."

"Wow! You really are wound up," Eric removed his suit jacket and carefully placed it over the back of a sleek leather office chair. He took a seat across from Stafford's desk. "It's tragic, but it happens. You can't let it get to you."

"I know it happens. Occasionally. And for a reason. Solid medical reasons."

"Nothing's turned up?"

"No. I have to wait for the autopsy." She shook her head. "Everything seemed normal, right up until it was time to deliver, and then all hell broke loose. It was like a bomb exploding. Everything happened so fast. Spasms.... Vomiting.... Intense pain, judging from all the screaming. It was horrific. I've never seen a body wracked with that much pain without any trauma or preexisting disease. Tachycardia. Arrhythmia. Blood pressure through the roof." She turned away. "And none if it makes any sense."

"The lab work didn't find anything?"

"No. Everything up until the delivery was completely normal. I'm hoping the post-mortem lab results will show something significant."

"There's a reason. There's always a reason. You just need to keep looking."

"What if I don't find anything?"

"Then look again. Get some consults. A fresh set of eyes may help. You were close to this patient. More so than most of the other mothers who've passed through your office door."

Stafford felt her throat become tense as she blurted out, "What are you insinuating, Eric? You think I'm not being objective? You think I'm too emotionally invested in this to find the cause of death?"

Eric's hands went up. "Whoa! That's not what I meant. I'm just saying; get a fresh set of eyes on it. That's all."

Stafford drew a breath and let her throat muscles relax. Then she spoke. "How about you, Eric? I know it's a little outside your field, but maybe you'll spot something?"

Eric settled back into his chair. "A *little* outside my field?" he chuckled. "I know obstetrics and orthopedics start with the same vowel." He grinned. "No. Anyone but me. Besides, I'm emotionally invested in this too." He leaned toward her. "There are plenty of other doctors in this hospital. They all respect you. Any one of them would be willing to look over all the labs and notes."

"I know you're right. It kills me. I promised Julie that this would be routine, like her first three pregnancies."

"I remember you talking about this case. Didn't you say that she had some second trimester symptoms?"

"Yes, but none of it indicative of this outcome." She shuffled around the reports on her desk then grabbed one of the printouts. "Julie's labs were fine. It was the fetus that had some abnormalities. I was so focused on Julie's charts that I forgot about the baby." She scanned the report. "Yes, here... the multiple marker screening. It had come back abnormal."

"See? Progress. You just needed a fresh set of eyes. Even if they're from ortho." Eric grinned. "So, the fetus had some genetic defect?"

"That's just it. Yes, and no. The results were abnormal, but they didn't indicate any one particular defect. Besides, why should that have affected Julie? A fetus with these particular genetic defects wouldn't have caused any serious symptoms in the mother. They certainly wouldn't have killed her."

"Tell me about these multiple defects."

"The markers individually were out of range, but grouped together, none of the marker patterns pointed to any known disease or genetic pattern of defects." Her eyes followed the list of acronyms and abbreviations along with their corresponding results. She read some of them aloud. "AFP, hCG, inhibin A, estriol, all slightly off, but not in any combination that made sense. At first I thought the tests were performed incorrectly, but we repeated them and got the same weird results."

"What about the amnio results?" He asked.

She looked up. "There was no amnio performed."

Eric's eyes widened. "With all the markers out-of-range, you didn't perform an amniocentesis? That's normal procedure."

"I couldn't. She wouldn't give consent."

"What? The patient didn't consent even after seeing those marker results." His eyes narrowed. "You did discuss the results with her, didn't you?"

Leslie dropped the report back onto her desk. "Of course I discussed the results with her. I remember it vividly now. She fainted in my exam room after hearing the news. I tried again a week later."

"Then why no consent?" He crossed his arms and leaned back in his chair. "She wasn't one of those anti-vaccine nutcases, was she?"

"Of course not! Julie was the surrogate mother. Gestational surrogate, not biological. She told me the donor parents wouldn't allow the procedure. I don't know why, but I remember that it was explicitly stated in the surrogacy agreement."

"I'm remembering more about this case. You told me that the donor parents skipped out on her? Isn't that why she came to you?"

"Yes, and no." Leslie waved a hand. "During her second trimester, Julie told me that she couldn't contact the medical facility that had done the IVF and implant, and that had been monitoring her health and the progress of the pregnancy. When she tried to call the parents, she was contacted by their attorney, who told her that they were overseas on business."

"They didn't have a cell phone? Sounds a bit sketchy if you ask me."

She nodded. "Yes it does. However, the attorney had the power to make decisions in the absence of the parents. The surrogacy agreement was very detailed. Our legal department cleared it so there wasn't much I could do."

"What about the patient? Doesn't her health and well-being trump a piece of paper?"

"That's the thing. There was nothing medically wrong with Julie. Her health was not in question. She wasn't in any danger. It was the fetus that may have had problems."

"And you couldn't intervene?"

"No. There's no law that says a mother must undergo any procedure if there is the possibility of birth defects. And since Julie was only the gestational surrogate, the biological parents' rights hold. It was their decision."

"Where are the parents now?"

"I don't know. They never got back to Julie after they disappeared during the second trimester. The attorney's gone missing, too."

"And what about the infant? Did it live?"

"When we realized that Julie couldn't be revived, we performed an emergency C-section. It's in the nursery now."

"In the nursery? Not in NICU?" Eric scratched his forehead. "I thought you said the baby had genetic birth defects? Why is it in the nursery and not in neonatal intensive care?"

"No, the baby was fine. Good birth weight, normal APGAR." Leslie paused. "Electrolytes were a little off, but other than that...." She shrugged. "I'm told that she's a hungry little thing. Sucked down several ounces of formula within a couple of hours. That's why I've ignored those previous genetic tests. The baby's health appears normal."

"There was nothing odd about the infant at all?"

Stafford thought a moment. "Well, it *was* a bit hairy," she chuckled. "And I remember one of the nurses remarking that there was a lot of caseosa, but there really wasn't that much. I didn't find it all that unusual. The pregnancy was at thirty-six weeks. Four weeks early."

Eric raised an eyebrow. "And it went straight to the nursery?"

"Everything about it was normal. Amazingly, there was no fetal distress during the entire ordeal." She paused. "The one other thing that was unusual, and what I'm waiting for from pathology, is an analysis of the cord and placenta."

"Why's that?" Eric asked.

"The cord was long," Stafford responded. "I mean, really long." She held her hands out, wide apart. "Maybe twice the length of a normal cord. I'm amazed that the baby didn't get tangled in it. I sent it to pathology for a complete work-up." She pointed at her desk. "It's the one big piece of information that's missing from this whole puzzle."

"How would that have affected the mother?"

"It shouldn't have. I don't see any connection."

Eric shifted in his chair. "You said the parents and the attorney are missing. Is the child going into foster care?"

"Yeah, most likely. Julie had no family," Leslie replied.

"That's too bad. Foster care can be a crapshoot."

Stafford leaned against the edge of her desk. "Yesterday, I was upstairs in the nursery to discuss dietary modifications for the baby. I met an army guy. A Colonel John Birchwood. He claimed that he was an old friend of Julie's family. Served with her dad. He said he could help arrange an adoption with another military family."

"That's good, right?"

"It seems a bit convenient, if you ask me."

"It's not that unusual. Relatives and friends often take in orphaned children."

"There's something about him that I don't trust. I can't put my finger on it. He had this southern accent."

"You don't trust southerners?" Eric chuckled.

"No, silly," she smirked. "The accent seemed... fake. Forced. One of the nurses on my staff, Melanie Connor, has a southern accent. She and her husband both grew up in Alabama before they moved here. This guy's accent wasn't the same." She pursed her lips and fluttered her eyelids. "He sounded like one of those proper southern plantation gentlemen, all charmin' with all the flowery language and all," she drawled and then rolled her eyes. "He just seemed fake."

Eric laughed. "Well, there are differences in southern accents. Plus, you can hardly consider yourself an expert on regional dialects. You can't get some of our own local idioms correct, and you grew up here," he grinned.

"It was more than that. He pretended to know about Julie. But he acted as if this was Julie's baby; like he didn't know that Julie was a surrogate." Stafford shook her head. "There's something about him I don't trust. It seemed like he was trying to pump me for info. I'm glad I used that interruption app you told me about. '*The Great Escape, Rescue Me*'. I set it on my smartphone before I started talking to him."

"Did you call security?"

"What? And accuse him of being *charmin*?"

The desk phone rang behind her. She twisted around and grabbed the handset. "Stafford here…. Yes…. Okay…. Tell me when you do have the results. Thank you." She placed the handset back into its cradle.

"What happened?" Eric asked.

"That was pathology returning my call. The report is delayed. Won't be ready until tomorrow."

"Isn't there a rush on it?"

"My case is a post mortem. Live patients' samples get priority. They share the same lab and staff. I hate saying that this is a routine death, but it's not a murder investigation. I'll have to wait."

"No, you don't. I'm sure there's some preliminary results. You don't have to wait for the official report." Eric leaned forward. "Why are you so invested in this patient?"

"I owe it to her. In some ways, it's my fault that this has happened to her."

"You can't blame yourself. You didn't do anything wrong. People get sick. They get injured. They have diseases and medical problems. Sometimes they die, despite all the medical knowledge you can bring to bear, they die. It's not your fault. You're a good doctor."

"It's my fault she was carrying this baby in the first place."

"Huh? What are you talking about?"

Stafford sunk into the plush leather chair across from Eric. "I first met Julie some years ago. She was alone, single. She had been raped and became pregnant. At the time I was doing some volunteer work at a free clinic. She came to me. At first I assumed that she wanted an abortion, but then I could see that there was something else. For some reason I befriended her. I don't know why. She was like a little lost puppy. Anyway, we talked. She couldn't support a child. She was single, struggling. She could barely support herself. But she also didn't want to give the baby away. It was a part of her. She wanted to know that it would have a good home, and not get passed around in the foster care system."

Eric leaned forward in his chair. "I didn't know this."

"It was way before we met," Leslie said. "I was starting to specialize in IVF and fertility treatments at that time. There was a couple I was trying to treat. They were young, successful, affluent. They had everything, except a child. They simply could not get pregnant. There were serious issues with his sperm. And her uterus wasn't up to the task. They couldn't accept it. I counseled them to consider adopting a child. At first they wouldn't consider it. Too many unknowns."

Eric shrugged. "Having a child is never a sure thing, whether it's yours or an adoption."

"Julie and I talked. I told her of this wonderful couple that was trying to have a baby. I told her that they were stuck on having their own child, but couldn't."

Eric raised an eyebrow. "You introduced them to each other?"

"It was Julie who actually hatched the plan," Leslie responded. "She asked me to contact the couple. I told them about Julie's plight. They agreed to meet each other. Julie and the other woman just clicked. It was like they were sisters. The couple paid for all of Julie's medical care. She moved into their home. They paid her a stipend. It worked out quite well. From there, I introduced Julie to other wealthy childless couples. She became a professional surrogate." Leslie paused. "I introduced her to that life."

Eric sat forward and waved his hands. "Wait a minute. Time out. Are you telling me that she was a surrogate for hire?"

"Yes. It's how she made a living."

"She sold her body to make babies for rich couples?"

"Yes."

Eric threw up his hands. "I can't believe you. You turned her into a prostitute."

"She was not a prostitute. She was a surrogate for hire. It's perfectly legal."

"Maybe in this state, but not others. Certainly not in most enlightened first world countries, or even in some third world countries."

Stafford raised a finger. "It was Julie's decision to become a surrogate multiple times. No one forced her into it."

Eric's eyes grew wide. "No one forced her into it? That's your defense?" He shook his head. "Are you listening to yourself? You're a doctor. You're supposed to be helping people stay healthy. To make healthy decisions." Eric paused. "Was she the only one?"

Stafford hesitated. "There are others."

"Are? You mean this is still going on? How many?"

"It varies. I introduce women who wish to be surrogates to wealthy childless couples. They pay all the surrogate's expenses and provide a place to live during the pregnancy. In exchange, the couple is guaranteed a young, healthy surrogate properly matched to the genetics of the biological parents. The pre-screenings that I do assure a mutually beneficial match for surrogate and biological parents and minimal complications for the pregnancy and birth."

"I can't believe what I'm hearing. There's that much of a demand for surrogates and that many wealthy childless couples in this city?"

"It's not only in Rapid City."

"What?"

"The parents are from all over. They contact me, arrange meetings with potential surrogates. When a match is made, the surrogates leave here to live with the parents during the pregnancy."

"And what do you get out of it?"

"I receive an introduction fee."

"An introduction fee? That's what you call it?" Eric stood. "I can't believe you do this. No wonder you never told me about it." He waved toward the wall of photographs. "I was always impressed with your work. In what you do, helping couples realize their dreams of having children. Now I learn that you've been making money by pimping out the wombs of destitute women. I can't believe it." He turned away from her, but his arm swept the room. "How could I have been so blind? All this fancy furniture. The seven-series BMW." He looked down at himself. "My suit...."

"Eric. Please." Stafford tried to calm him. "Please listen. I'm doing good work. Why can't I do good and also deserve to be good to myself, too?"

"Why is it always about the money with you?" Eric shot back. "I thought I knew you, but I don't. The more I see what's going on around you, the things you do, the people you're talking to, your business dealings, the more I realize that I don't know this person."

He circled his chair, then said. "How old are you? Now I understand why you've never been married; never had a long term relationship. I used to think that was all gossip from other women jealous of your professional success; finding anything to tear you down. Turns out, they didn't have to look too far. I'm the one who's been blind. You're trying to buy me with fancy suits and dinners like you try to buy everything else. I'm not a commodity. You can't buy my love and affection, Leslie." He turned away from her and faced the wall of smiling new parents.

"Please. Eric. Let me explain."

He drew a long breath, and then turned back to her. "With all your supposedly careful matching and screening, how do you explain what happened with Julie?"

"I can't. Julie went freelance on me. I was not involved in the introduction. Julie came to me only after the parents disappeared during her second trimester. She didn't know what happened to them."

"So, because of you, there are no parents, an orphaned child, and a dead mother." He turned away from her and stared at the collage of parents and infants on the wall. "You need to find out what killed her. It's the least you can do." He spun around to face

Stafford. "And you need to find the surrogate parents. That baby deserves a good home." Eric grabbed his suit jacket, brushed past Stafford and headed for the door.

"Eric. Wait, please!"

She watched him leave. She stood, motionless, staring at the open door.

He's right. Julie's dead because of me. I owe it to her, and to the baby, to find out what happened.

She grabbed her purse off her desk, dropped it in a drawer and locked it.

I'm going down to pathology to find out what's holding up the reports. They must have looked at the body by now. It's been a couple of days already. If there's any data that will help me solve this, I want it now.

TUESDAY,
8:47 AM MDT

"Hey, Stark."

Doctor Daniel Stark looked up from his laptop. He pushed his wire glasses back into place from the tip of his nose.

"Stark. I'm heading down to radiology. Keep an eye on the two new technicians for me, please."

Stark spun around on his bench stool. Even sitting, he was face to face with his shorter, older colleague. He blinked one eye, then the other. "Left or right?"

Sanders groaned. "Stark, your jokes are no better here than when we worked together at the morgue."

"No worse, either. Can't fault me for being consistent." He smiled.

Sanders shook his head. Just make sure the techs don't need anything for those samples they're prepping. I'll be down at radiology.

Stark watched his boss leave, then glanced around the pathology lab. The two lab techs were busy prepping and running tests on the onslaught of blood, urine, and biopsy specimens that had poured in over the last twenty four hours. This was an unusual amount of lab work in such a short period of time. He wasn't aware of any major accidents or other calamity that would have caused such a spike. The lab was also behind on completing an autopsy. He and Doctor Marc Sanders were the only two pathologists on duty and the only ones qualified to perform the procedure.

Stark checked his watch then ducked into the lab's small conference room, closed the door and drew closed the window blinds. He punched in a phone number on the conference phone that sat on the round wooden table. Its speaker burbled as the connection was made.

A blast of noise shot from the phone's speaker. It sounded like a chorus of high powered fans. Stark could barely understand the voice buried beneath it.

Stark shouted back at the phone. "Blake? Is that you? I can't hear you. What's all that noise?"

There was a sharp click on the line, then silence. After a moment, Blake Farnsworth's crisp, clear voice emerged from the speaker. There was no trace of the background windstorm.

"Daniel? Hey buddy, how's it going?"

"Blake. Where are you? What was all that noise?"

"Sorry. We had the door open. The view is astounding. Wish you were here to see it."

"Huh? You're driving with the doors open?"

"No, no. I'm in a helicopter. I'm on a ski trip. Heli-Skiing."

"What? Where the hell are you skiing this time of year? Wait - are you even in the country?"

"I'm at Bighorn at Revelstoke, British Columbia. Helluva snow pack this season. So, what's up? I've got a few minutes before we reach the summit jump off point."

"Huh? Jump off point?"

"Yeah. The 'copter flies us up to the summit. We all jump out and ski down the slope. It's sheer exhilaration."

"Sounds more like a death wish. Listen. I found some Neanderthal DNA."

"Yeah, I know. You found that months ago. What's your point?"

"My point is that I found new DNA. It's a different individual, but it's Neanderthal."

There was silence on the line. Then Farnsworth spoke in a hushed tone. "Are you certain?"

"Yes! I'm certain. And even better than that, it's a newborn."

"A newborn baby with Neanderthal DNA?"

"Yeah, and not just traces of Neanderthal DNA like we all have. This is close to one hundred percent pure." The grin on Stark's face nearly followed his voice's excitement through the phone line. "It's a newborn Neanderthal."

Again, silence on the line. Then Farnsworth spoke. "This is bad. They must have successfully impregnated some female. I assume it was a human female host?"

"Yeah, of course. That's how babies are made." Stark shook his head. "The mother died during childbirth, but I got to perform the autopsy. I've got her specimens and I've been hanging on to the lab results." Stark leaned toward the conference phone and blurted into the microphone. "Farnsworth, we have a real, live Neanderthal here at my hospital. How cool is that?"

"Daniel, calm down for a minute."

"Why? This is groundbreaking. A real, live, Neanderthal. And I discovered it!" Stark pranced around the conference room table, waving his arms. "I'm gonna be famous!"

Farnsworth's voice bellowed from the speakerphone. "Daniel! Listen to me."

Stark stopped his prancing. "What?"

"What about the newborn? Did it live? Do you have the body?" Farnsworth asked.

"No... I mean yes... I mean...." Stark drew a breath and exhaled slowly. "No. I don't have the body. The baby is alive and healthy. It's in the hospital nursery."

"Has anyone figured it out?"

"No. Not as far as I know. I'm sure that if they knew it was a Neanderthal baby the news would be all over the place."

Stark could hear muffled shouts come across the phone line. It sounded like someone barking orders. Then Farnsworth was back. "I'm coming there."

Stark took a seat next to the speaker phone and rested his arms on the polished surface of the conference table. "Why? I thought you were skiing in, well, wherever you are?"

"This is too important. I'm going to ruin a few folks' ski trip, but, hell, there's no way I can ski now with this on my mind."

"That's real nice of you to do, Blake. But you don't have to cut your vacation short for me. Besides, it's going to be a few days before I finish writing the article and submit it for publication. You have plenty of time to hell-ski, or whatever it's called, and then come here. Just don't kill yourself."

Farnsworth's voice was stern. "Daniel. Listen to me. Bury those lab results. No one can see them. No one."

Stark stared and blinked at the speaker phone. "Why?"

"Listen, Daniel. That mother is dead for a reason. The people who impregnated her with that Neanderthal are going to come looking for it. And they're not going to be nice."

"Shit! Are you saying that the military's going to be coming after me?"

"They only want the baby. All I can say is that it's best you stay out of it and not attract attention. Can you do that?"

"I'll try. But I can't stall for that long. The doctor who ordered the reports and the autopsy has already been waiting too long. I can't stall her forever." He looked around the empty room, leaned close to the phone and whispered, "She can be a real bitch."

"Stall as long as possible. I'll get there as soon as I can."

Stark's voice went up an octave or two. "Do you realize what you're asking me to do? I can't simply drop the reports in the trash and pretend that nobody asked for them. There's an active investigation about the mother's death. I've got the doctor who ordered the tests breathing down my neck." Stark's voice started to crack. "Somebody died. I'm not sure how long I can keep this a secret." He paused to catch his breath, then asked, "Wait. You're going to catch a flight back here just like that?"

"You forget, my friend. I have a private plane. I'll be there before you know it."

Stark let out some air. "Right. Okay. I'll stall as long as I can. But that doctor is more of a pain than Sanders. She's going to corner me at some point."

"Just hang on. I'll be there soon enough."

The call terminated with a click.

Stark stared at the silent phone. He removed his glasses and rubbed his eyes. The click of the conference room door opening behind him made him snap to attention. He spun around. It was Sanders.

"Um, hi Boss," Stark stammered. "How was radiology? Any new tunes?"

Sanders closed the door, crossed his arms and glared. "Knock it off, Stark. Did I hear what I think I heard?"

"Don't know. What did you hear?"

"That was Farnsworth on the phone, right?"

"Um, yeah. He's skiing. Heli-skiing. Crazy, eh?"

"Did I hear the words 'Neanderthal' and 'DNA' come out of your mouth?"

Stark regained his composure. "Were you eavesdropping? That was a private conversation."

"If you were making a private call, you should have used your cell phone." Sanders pointed at the speaker phone. "That's hospital property. It's in my lab. Therefore it's my business."

"Come on, Boss. You know that cell reception is lousy in this lab. I would have had to go outside. That would have taken more time. See. Using the conference room phone was more efficient." Stark grinned. "And I know how you cherish efficiency. You should be happy."

Sanders let his arms drop. He shook his head and gritted his teeth. Finally, he spoke, "I don't know why I took this job. If I had known that this is where you came after leaving the morgue, I would never have even applied for the position."

Stark stood. He put a hand on Sander's shoulder. "I think you missed me. I heard it got really quiet at the morgue after I left. The clientele were kind of tight-lipped about it but the interns emailed me a few times. Said it was like working at, well, you know, a morgue." He grinned.

"Excuse me!" A brassy female voice sliced through their bickering. Sanders spun around and nearly planted his nose into the cleavage of an attractive young blonde woman dressed in rumpled forest green scrubs. He stumbled back, red-faced and wide-eyed.

Stark snickered, and before Sanders had a chance to speak, Stark stepped between them. "Doctor Stafford. Nice to see you again." Stark extended an arm toward the lab area in an attempt to get Stafford away from his boss. "Let's go over to my desk and I'll try to assist you."

Stafford held her ground. "Don't try to stall, Stark. I'm looking for my lab results. And the autopsy report. I know you have them. What's the hold-up?"

"I don't usually see you dressed-down, Doctor Stafford," Stark replied. "Where's your designer dress and high heels?" He glanced at his watch. "Is it casual Friday?"

Stafford's eyes became daggers. A scowl crossed her face. "Drop the comedy act, Stark. I do actually work. With patients. In delivery rooms. I don't wear Prada to a pregnancy," she sneered.

Sanders frowned at Stark, then turned and smiled at Stafford. "Don't pay attention to him. How can I help you, Doctor?"

"And who are you? His sidekick?"

Stark chimed in. "Doctor Leslie Stafford, meet Doctor Marc Sanders." Then he added, "Doctor Sanders is the new lab manager."

Stafford turned back to face Sanders. "You're Stark's boss? Finally, progress." She crossed her arms and stared through him. "Where are my lab reports? I'm looking for some blood chemistry results. And I requested pathology to examine a placenta. There's also the matter of an autopsy for a deceased patient."

Sanders extended an arm motioning toward his office across the lab. "Please. Follow me, Doctor. I'll look up the lab results now." Stark watched as they walked away. He smiled and shook his head, then went across to the other end of the lab. He washed and dried his hands, grabbed a clean pair of latex gloves from the dispenser, then began prepping some blood samples for analysis.

Minutes later, he heard someone shout his name. He looked around.

"Stark!"

Stark looked across the lab and saw Sanders waving for him to join Stafford and him in his office. Stark smiled and waved back. Sanders scowled and his mouth slowly and clearly formed the words: *Come. Here. Now.* Stark pulled off his gloves and tossed them into the biohazard bin. He jogged over to Sanders' office. Sanders was standing in the doorway with his arms crossed. A frown covered his face.

Stark smiled and asked, "What's up, Boss?"

Sanders pointed at a laptop on his desk. The screen displayed a spreadsheet listing lab tests and results. "These reports are ready. Why aren't these lab results released?"

"I was double checking the data. There were some anomalies. I wanted to make sure that all the lab work was done properly."

"What anomalies?"

"That's why I was talking with Blake."

Both of Sander's hands went up. He shook his head. "No, no, no, no. Stark. You're not back to those military cloning conspiracies again."

"It's not a conspiracy. It's real. Don't you remember what happened last year? Remember, that dead professor with Neanderthal DNA?"

Stafford looked at Stark, then back at Sanders. "What the hell are you two talking about? Military conspiracy? Neanderthal DNA? What's that got to do with my patient?"

Stark bit his lip. "The baby is a Neanderthal," he blurted.

Stafford blinked and stared at Stark. "What?"

"The genetics, the genome, its DNA. It's Neanderthal, not Homo sapiens."

"OK, now you're being an idiot," Stafford snapped. "I know you have a thing for me, Stark. You're always making up some excuse to get me down here. Cut the crap and tell me the truth."

"I am telling the truth."

Sanders grabbed Stark by the arm and pulled him away from Stafford and toward a corner of his office. "Stark, we're not going to do this all over again, are we?"

Stafford followed them. "Do what all over again?"

Sanders took a breath, swallowed, then said, "Last year, he got this crazy idea that a body that came through the morgue had Neanderthal DNA. He got involved with some rich playboy with nothing better to do but play espionage games."

"It wasn't a game! Do you remember the news last year about the law firm that was secretly impregnating prostitutes?"

Sanders scratched his forehead. "How could they secretly impregnate prostitutes? Wouldn't the women notice that they were pregnant?"

Stafford looked at Stark and rolled her eyes. "Now I understand why you still have your job." She took a breath and turned back to Sanders. "Yes, I remember the story. The news reports said they were hiring the prostitutes to be surrogates and then were selling the babies on the black market."

"Oh. That still sounds illegal," Sanders replied.

Stafford turned away from Sanders and mouthed the word 'moron'. Stark smiled and shrugged back at her. She turned back to Sanders, let out a sigh and said, "Yes, that's why the government shut them down. Arrested all the high level officers; the board of directors. Closed down the company." She turned to Stark. "You know more about what happened?"

"Um, yeah," Stark replied. "There was some experimentation that was going on. Cloning."

"Cloning babies?" Stafford asked.

"No, cloning Neanderthals."

Sanders jumped back into the conversation. "There you go again with the Neanderthal thing."

"It's true!" Stark exclaimed. "The company was working with the military to clone Neanderthals."

Sanders moved to usher Stark out of his office, but Stafford put up her hand and asked, "Why would they want to do that?"

"As soldiers," Stark replied. "Untraceable soldiers that no one would miss when they were killed in battle."

"But why Neanderthals? Why not humans?"

"Apparently there were other characteristics of Neanderthals that made them superior soldiers," Stark responded. Then he added, "Plus, they were cannibals."

Both Sanders and Stafford gasped. "What?"

Stark tried to look as serious as possible. "Cannibals. Once deployed, the 'Thals, as they called them, would not need to be supplied. That was their motivation for the mission. They would hunt down and eat the enemy."

Stafford looked right at him. "You're nuttier than I thought."

He raised his right hand. "It's true. I swear."

"So, you're telling me that the army was planning to clone a bunch of Neanderthals, and then drop them behind enemy lines where they would feast on the enemy?"

Stark nodded. "Yeah, that's essentially it."

Stafford looked at him sideways. "I think I saw that movie."

"Those weren't Neanderthals, they were...."

Stafford nearly bit off Stark's head. "Oh, shut up, Stark! Can I get my lab reports? Now!"

"Yes, Stark, you're wasting the good doctor's time," Sanders added.

"Fine. I'll release the reports," Stark huffed. "You can believe what you want but the science doesn't lie." He pointed toward the ceiling, looked directly at both of them and said, "That baby is a Neanderthal."

"Yeah, and I'm a Kardashian," Stafford remarked as she walked out the office door. She called over her shoulder, "Just send me the reports."

Stark called after her, "Doctor Stafford. What color are the baby's eyes?"

Stafford stopped in her tracks. She spun around. "How did you know the infant's sclera had pigment?"

"I told you, I did a DNA analysis."

"That doesn't mean it's Neanderthal," Stafford scoffed. "It's more likely melanosis. Geez, Stark, don't you ever give up?" She looked at Sanders. "How do you put up with him?"

"He can be a pain, but he's a damn fine pathologist," Sanders fired back. He crossed his arms, pursed his lips and, despite the height difference, stared silently at Stafford.

"Just get me my lab reports," she huffed as she turned on her heel and strutted back down the hallway toward the elevator.

The two men watched her walk away. They stood silent for a moment. Stark turned his head and watched Sanders as his eyes followed Stafford down the corridor. Then he spoke. "Hey, thanks for sticking up for me. You really cut her down to size."

Sanders, his eyes still locked on the retreating Doctor Stafford, mumbled something.

Stark nudged his boss with an elbow. "She could be a Kardashian."

Sanders snapped his head around to face Stark. "What? What are you talking about, Stark?"

"Her ass. I saw you checking her out. I'll bet you were mentally balancing a champagne flute on her backside."

Sanders blushed and sputtered. "I was doing no such thing."

"Probably for the best anyway," Stark patted Sander's shoulder a couple of times. As he left Sander's office to return to his interrupted lab work, he added, "Besides, she's way out of your league."

"Don't make me regret what I said, Stark. Now get back to work."

WEDNESDAY,
8:23 AM MDT

Doctor Leslie Stafford sat at her desk staring intently at her laptop. She clicked the mouse a few times, scrolled the screen up, then down, then clicked again. Her eyes narrowed a bit as she leaned in closer to read a PDF that had popped up in the browser. She moved the mouse's scroll wheel a little at a time. At times her lips formed partial words from the document as she read. She reached the bottom of the document, blinked a few times, then leaned back, keeping her fingers poised near the keyboard.

Glancing around at the piles of folders on her desk, she reached over one pile and grabbed a manila folder adorned with multicolored tags along its tab. She pushed away the laptop, opened the folder in front of her, and leafed through lab reports and printouts until she stopped at one single sheet.

Damn. He's right.

She flipped over the sheet and kept reading.

I can't believe that he's right about this. I wonder what else he knows.

She started leafing through the rest of the folder when her desk phone chimed. "Doctor Leslie Stafford," she answered. She coddled the handset to an ear with her shoulder while trying to sort through the remaining pages within the folder.

"They don't have an appointment? What is it that they want to see me about?"

She could hear muffled voices at the other end as some questions were asked and answered, then the receptionist's voice returned. Stafford's hands froze in midair over the folder. She grabbed the handset that was jammed between her shoulder and ear and stood. Her wheeled chair skidded backwards and clattered against the polished ebony finish of a credenza.

"Yes, please, send them to my office immediately. Thank you."

Stafford scooped up the mess of folders and shoved them back into the open drawer of the mahogany task cabinet that stood in the back corner of her office. She pulled a pair of three inch Ivanka Trump pumps out from under her desk, jammed her feet into them, smoothed the wrinkles of her Armani Collezioni long sleeve Milano jersey dress, then settled back into her chair. She closed her laptop and pushed it aside, leaving a bare, glossy expanse of the desk between her and her office door.

There was a knock at the door.

"Please, come in."

The door opened and Stafford stood to greet the well-dressed young couple that entered her office.

Stafford eyed the young blonde woman.

Who dressed her this morning? That drop-waist dress does nothing for her figure. I do like what she's done with her hair, though. I might have to try that.

Stafford studied the stranger's face closely. There was something oddly familiar about her. Yes, she had seen this woman before. It was on Monday, when she was up in the maternity ward hallway with Birchwood. She had noticed this same woman come out of the elevator, freeze for a couple of seconds, then lurch back in.

"Have we met before?" she asked, and watched the woman's facial expressions as she responded.

"Um, no. I don't think so?" The blonde glanced at her partner then smiled back at Stafford.

Stafford pressed her a bit. "I'm sorry. I thought I spotted you a couple of days ago in the maternity ward."

"Um, no. That wasn't me." The blonde head turned back toward her partner and made a bit of a face. Stafford wondered why this woman was lying.

"Yes, couldn't have been," added the gentleman. He wore an untailored Armani suit. "We've only arrived back in the states yesterday. Still a bit jet lagged. We were in Europe on some business. I'm sorry; we've not even introduced ourselves. I'm James Williams and this is my wife, Linda."

Stafford extended a hand and motioned toward the two Italian leather armchairs in front of her desk.

"Please. Have a seat."

Stafford kept one eye on the blonde woman as she sat herself behind her sleek Karim Rashid desk. Its bare, expansive glass desktop served as a figurative moat between her and this suspicious couple.

Stafford got right down to business. "I was told that you are trying to contact one of my patients?" Stafford glanced back and forth at the two, watching their eyes. "How do you know Julie?"

The blonde spoke. "Um, Julie was carrying my, I mean our child." She turned and smiled at her husband.

Stafford caught the husband wincing, just a bit. She hesitated.

He's bothered by something the blonde said. Something is not right here.

She addressed them both. "I don't understand. She's carrying your child and now you don't know where she is?"

Stafford saw the blonde's mouth open to speak, but her husband's hand moved quickly, landing on the blonde's thigh and giving it a firm squeeze as he began speaking. "We were out of the country on some business for a short time. When we returned, we couldn't contact her. Phone calls and emails went unanswered. She had stopped visiting the doctor we had arranged for her to see for prenatal care."

The blonde shook her head and smiled.

Stafford kept trying to size up these two odd-acting people.

There's something funny about these two.

"I'm curious how you found me?" she asked.

"Our doctor had some of Julie's medical records that had been forwarded to him from this hospital," the husband responded, his hand still firmly planted on the blonde's thigh.

I would have known about any of Julie's records being sent out.

She allowed him to continue speaking.

"We're very concerned, not only for Julie, but for the child…" He glanced at his blonde partner. "… our child, that she's carrying."

Something's not adding up.

"You realize that I'm bound by doctor/patient confidentiality. I can't reveal any personal information. However, I certainly can pass along your contact information to her."

"We're hoping that you could help us find her. You may be bound by doctor/patient confidentiality, but that applies, if at all, to you and Julie. The unborn child is ours and we have parental rights." The husband paused and stared at Stafford. "We thought perhaps that she visited you for prenatal checkups during her second trimester."

He's fishing, trying to figure out what I know. I've got to be careful about what I say. What else are they hiding?

"I can tell you that Julie has been my patient in the past, but I can't tell you when we've met or for what reason."

Stafford leaned back in her chair, cocked her head slightly and laid her arms on the chair's contoured armrests. She hoped that this body language would dampen the husband's implied aggressiveness.

"I understand your concern and your predicament. I see a lot of parents who go the surrogacy route. It's not easy; giving up control of your unborn child to another woman."

Stafford paused and watched the couples' eyes.

No reaction from either of them. Usually there's some hint of surrogate jealousy by one of the parents.

Stafford smiled and resumed speaking. "The dynamics can be confusing at times. I was not involved in the original surrogacy arrangements or fertilization. I'm not sure how much help I can be."

The husband spoke. "Perhaps Julie may have given birth to our child, here, prematurely." It didn't sound like a question.

Stafford's body tensed.

Shit! That came out of nowhere. They know more than they're letting on. How the hell am I supposed to respond to a comment like that?

Stafford thought for a moment, then said, "If Julie is a patient at this hospital, you can certainly request to visit her during normal visiting hours. Other than that…" she shrugged.

"Is Julie dead?" the husband asked, his eyes locked on Stafford's.

Stafford struggled to maintain an outward air of composure while her mind raced.

Damn. They know. Or do they? Nothing about Julie's death has been released publicly. Do they have someone on the inside giving them information? Julie has no family. She had no visitors here. The only people who know that she died are the hospital staff. They wouldn't have told anyone, not by name at least.

She thought back to that tense day: Julie's deadly reaction to the birth; the emergency C-section. No one had come to visit her or claim her body.

Birchwood! That military guy. He was here the day after Julie died. He was more interested in the child than Julie.

She eyed the couple sitting before her. The way that the husband sat there in his chair was the epitome of a man in charge. The blonde however, …. Stafford thought back to their brief hallway encounter.

It wasn't the sight of me that sent this bitch scurrying back into the elevator. It was Birchwood. Are they working together or are they rivals? Or do they even know about him? They didn't introduce themselves as military.

Stafford allowed her body to relax.

Time for me to do some fishing of my own.

"Do you know Colonel Birchwood?" she asked.

The tension in the room became palpable. Stafford caught the blonde as she bit her lip for the briefest moment before recovering her composure.

Gotcha!

Stafford cocked her head slightly and revealed a touch of a smile, waiting for the couple to respond.

The three adults stared at each other. Stafford watched the blonde look at her supposed husband and saw her squeeze his hand. He spoke. "Colonel Birchwood?"

Don't play with me. I bet you know the Colonel. And something's telling me that you don't want him here.

"Yes, he was here on Monday."

The blonde sat, stone-still. Stafford waited for a response. The husband shifted in his seat.

Stafford broke the pregnant pause. "One of the nurses told me that this Colonel Birchwood was Julie's only visitor," Stafford lied. She paused, waiting for some reaction, then shifted the conversation. "Tell me. What surrogacy agency introduced you to Julie?"

The husband hesitated. "It was a private arrangement. There was no agency."

Stafford let herself sink deeper into her chair's soft Italian leather.

I'm knocking him off his game.

"Oh? Did you already know Julie?"

"Um. No." The couple looked at each other. "We were introduced to her by a mutual friend."

Well that's bullshit.

"Maybe your friend knows where Julie is? I imagine that someone who knew Julie well enough to introduce her to you as a potential surrogate would still be in touch with her?"

"We had spoken to her," the husband answered, this time without any hesitation. "She didn't know what happened to Julie either. She told us that she and Julie had not spoken to each other for a few weeks."

The couple glanced at each other. The blonde squeezed her husband's hand again. "We're all very concerned," he said. The wide-eyed blonde kept quiet but smiled weakly and nodded.

Okay, they're just making up shit now. There's nothing more to learn from these two. I've got to get rid of them and do some digging on my own.

"Probably the best thing you can do at this point would be to file a missing-persons report with the police. They can help you more than I can."

Stafford stood, signaling the end of the conversation. "I wish I could help you more, but at this point it seems more like a job for the authorities. I understand what you're both going through." She glanced over at the wall covered with photos of beaming parents with their newborns. "I'm really sorry that you're in such a heart-rending situation and that I couldn't help more."

She came around her desk and extended her hands to the couple. "If I do learn anything, or if I hear from Julie, I'll let you know." She shook the husband's hand first, then the blonde's. Stafford placed her other hand on the blonde's, feigning concern, looked into the wide, vacant eyes and said, "You'll find your baby."

Stafford watched the couple leave her office, closing the door behind them. She returned to her desk, kicked off her pumps, flipped up the lid of her laptop, and brought up the browser.

She Googled keywords and phrases in various combinations, hoping for a hit that would reveal more information about this mysterious couple: 'James Williams', 'Linda Williams', 'Military', 'Wedding', 'Surrogate'. She found little. Too little in fact.

An upper middle class couple living in this area would have some sort of digital footprint: Facebook pages, LinkedIn accounts, Twitter handles. But there was nothing. Not even a wedding announcement in the local newspaper. It didn't help that their first and last names were common; all in the top five most common names in North America.

All this made it difficult for Stafford to filter through the digital clutter that Google dredged up as she tried to zero in on these two mysterious visitors. There was too much information and no hope of sorting through all of it.

Stafford leaned back, closed her eyes, and ran her fingers through her hair.

Feels dry. I don't like that new conditioner that my hair stylist switched to.

She rubbed her eyes, then sat up and typed three words, 'Colonel Birchwood Neanderthal', into the Google search entry field of her browser. She stared at the words, then hit the enter key.

Leaning in close, she read each of the results slowly. She clicked on one.

Her eyes grew wide at the colorful, eye-catching graphics that were displayed along with the short descriptive paragraphs, excerpts, and reviews by readers.

Stafford stopped reading and realized that her fists were clenched. She slowly stretched out her fingers and, keeping her palms firmly planted on the edge of her desk, she pushed herself deep into her chair and muttered, "Stark."

WEDNESDAY,
8:41 AM MDT

"Why didn't you tell me that was Julie's doctor that you saw speaking with Birchwood?" Bob said to Mary as they left Doctor Stafford's office and walked down the hospital's brightly lit hallway. Its beige-on-beige motif was adorned with framed posters declaring this to be a world-class medical center.

Bob stayed a couple of steps ahead of Mary as they headed to the elevator at the end of the hall. "I thought you had learned her name and looked her up on the hospital's website?"

Mary stopped walking, forcing Bob to stop in his tracks.

"How was I supposed to know?" she blurted. "I never met her before. The woman I saw two days ago in the maternity ward looked nothing like the Doctor Stafford that we just met."

She started to tick off the points she wanted to make on her fingers.

"This Doctor Stafford was fashionably dressed and had her hair all done up, like in the website photo. The woman that I saw talking to Birchwood looked like some E.R. nurse that had finished a grueling twelve hour shift. Besides, I didn't think that woman had paid attention to me ducking back into the elevator on Monday."

All five fingers of her hand were spread as she made her final point.

"Plus, I was much more focused on not being spotted by Birchwood. I wasn't concerned about being recognized by any of the hospital staff. They wouldn't have known who I was."

Bob glared at Mary, his hands on his hips. "Well, then, how did she get a good enough look at you that she recognized you again today?"

Mary's voice rose an octave, turning the heads of a smiling young couple that had squeezed by them. "I don't know. I must have stood there for a couple of seconds when I came out of the elevator and then spotted Birchwood." Her eyes began to well-up. "I'm sorry. I froze in my tracks I guess. She probably saw me staring at the two of them before I bolted back into the elevator before the doors closed." She wiped an eye. "I wanted to get out of there as fast as I could."

"What the hell's gotten into you lately? You're forgetting things, making novice mistakes. And look at the way you're dressed."

Mary looked down at herself, then back at Bob. "What's wrong with the way I'm dressed?"

"You could have worn something you already own, or even the outfit from our original meeting with Julie. Instead you went and spent a couple hundred dollars on this fancy dress. You can't expense that to the government and you certainly can't afford it out of your own pocket."

"I had to look the part."

"What part? What are you talking about? All you had to do was look and act like a worried adoptive mother, not some fashion model."

"I had to wear something like this. Did you see Stafford's photo? Did you see how she was dressed back there in her office? I wanted to level the playing field. I didn't want her to chew me up and spit me out. I wanted her to consider me her equal and to see that I earned this baby."

"Really? Seriously? Did you think that wearing these clothes was going to level the playing field and make it easier? You leveled the playing field all right. You played right into her psyche, like an arms race. She looked at you and saw competition, not a concerned parent. Jesus, Mary. You were supposed to make her feel sympathetic to our plight, not antagonistic. She's probably all screwed up trying to figure us out now. You may have dressed the part, but you didn't act the part. Meanwhile, I had to jump in and keep you from saying something stupid. It made me look like some overbearing, controlling husband who likes his wife to play dress-up like a Barbie doll."

"What? Now you think I'm stupid?"

"No, I don't think you're stupid. But I am concerned about how you've been acting the past few months. You seem to be in a fog sometimes. Not on top of your game. Is there something wrong? Something I should know about? He paused. "Wait, you're not pregnant are you?"

"No, I'm not pregnant."

"Okay, 'cause now you got me thinking that all your talk about adopting a baby was your way to ease me into the news."

"I had a miscarriage."

Bob wasn't sure that he heard that correctly. It took him a moment to sort out how he wanted to respond. He shook his head. "What? You had a miscarriage? When? You're just telling me this now?"

"It happened before we met. A year ago. I didn't tell anyone. No one even knew I was pregnant. Hell, I didn't know I was pregnant."

"How could you not know that you were pregnant?" He waggled a finger toward Mary's abdomen. "Wouldn't you have noticed your, um, …friend, not visiting on time?"

"I'm very irregular. I go weeks, months sometimes without a visit. Apparently you haven't noticed that either."

"But didn't you notice a little, … you know." He cupped his hand in a motion in front of his stomach.

"Oh, Bob, honey. I know you're attracted to me, but I'm not the thinnest woman in the world. It happened at four months. Some women don't start showing until then."

"I've got a lot to learn. Why didn't you tell anyone?"

"I didn't want my superiors to find out. I had started training for field ops. It wasn't the type of news I wanted going around."

"Did you at least see someone for, you know, …" He pointed at his head.

"Are you kidding? And then forced to have a psych eval? That definitely would have put my career on hold."

The elevator doors opened. A young couple stepped out. The man was carrying a sleeping infant in a brightly colored carrier. The woman was lugging an overstuffed diaper bag. Neither one of them were smiling. Bob stepped past them and into the waiting elevator. He reached to press the lobby button on the panel, then stopped. Mary was still standing in the hallway, watching the young family trudging down the hallway away from them. He cleared his throat. Mary snapped around, smiled, and drifted into the elevator. As the doors slid closed, Bob noticed her eyes fixed on the young parents receding down the corridor. He interrupted her thoughts with his question. "So why the change of heart now?"

"Huh? What do you mean?"

"You just told me that you hid your miscarriage from everyone and that you didn't want anything to derail your career. Now it seems that you're craving a baby so much that you want to adopt Julie's."

"I don't know. I can't explain it. It's like some other part of my brain has switched on."

"Maybe you should have talked to someone back then."

"Maybe this was all meant to be."

"All this what?"

"Julie dying. This orphaned child. Maybe it's a sign. Maybe I'm supposed to go down this path. Adopt this child. Raise it. Be a mother."

"I think you're reading way too much into all this, Mary. Besides, you just said having a child would derail your desire to become a field op."

"That's it. Maybe I'm not supposed to be a field op. Maybe God is trying to tell me something."

"Okay, now you're getting a little weird, Mary."

"You don't think God sends messages?"

"I think we're getting off topic. Right now I think we have to focus on getting custody of this child before Birchwood makes a move." Bob softened his tone a bit. "You've got a lot to learn about being a field operative. Like how to react to unexpected situations so that you don't give yourself away. Good thing I could cover for you with that lie about arriving back from Europe."

The elevator doors opened and they exited into the hospital's main lobby. As they made their way toward the exit, Bob asked, "Please tell me that you weren't in uniform when Stafford spotted you."

"Yes, No. I mean no, I wasn't in uniform."

"Good," Bob sighed. "Hopefully she doesn't make any connection between us and Birchwood. That would seriously complicate any chance of getting this baby to safety."

Mary spoke up. "What if she does make the connection?"

"I don't see how she could or would," Bob replied. "There's nothing obviously connecting us with Birchwood. We didn't say anything about being in the military. We only presented ourselves as would-be parents trying to find our child's gestational surrogate who's gone missing."

"What if Birchwood said something?" Mary asked.

"What do you mean?"

"What if he told Doctor Stafford about the project? Or mentioned our real names?" Mary's voice went up an octave. "Oh god! What if he told her that a couple pretending to be the surrogate parents would be coming to try kidnapping the baby?"

"Calm down, Mary. Your imagination is running wild again. Why would Birchwood do any of those things? He's got as much to lose as us. Maybe more."

"He must have told her something. I saw them talking."

"You saw them for a few short seconds. You have no idea what they were talking about. He could have been asking for directions. If their conversation was trivial she would not remember him as much as she remembered seeing a blonde woman walk out of the elevator, stare at her in surprise, and then rush back into the elevator."

Mary's voice became harsh. "You're making me feel like a real idiot, you know that, don't you? And you, blurting that out about Julie being dead. How would a real surrogate couple know about that? And wouldn't they have been a lot more upset if they knew that was true?"

"I was trying to push her off balance and get her to spill more information."

Mary crossed her arms. "It didn't work. She didn't say anything."

"I watched her body language. She tensed up. She knows what happened to Julie."

"And now she knows that we know, too. I don't see how this helps us."

Bob stopped short before they reached the main doors of the lobby. "I got her to admit that she had a memorable conversation with Birchwood. Now we know where he is and what he's up to. She would not have mentioned his name, or even remembered his name, if she didn't think there was some connection between us. She may think that we and Birchwood are rivals. That means she won't know who's acting in the infant's best interests. She doesn't know who to trust. That gives us the upper hand."

Mary grew quiet. She stared at her feet.

Bob placed a hand on her shoulder. "I'm sorry. I'm not trying to tear you down. I'm only trying to analyze all the facts and figure out our next move."

Mary looked up into Bob's eyes. "I'm sorry for doubting you, honey." She smiled. "What's our next move?"

"Not sure. I'm going to go with the worst case scenario. Birchwood is trying to kidnap the baby. He's probably doing some recon to assess the security weaknesses of this hospital. I would not be surprised if he comes here multiple times over the next few days to gather intel, learn the staff routines, memorize names and faces of the nurses. You said that you tailed him back to his motel?"

"Yeah. It's a couple of miles from here."

"Looks like I'm going to have to do some recon of my own."

"What are you talking about? Wait. You're not going to follow Birchwood around, are you?"

"I think I need to. I have to figure out what he's up to."

"You told me yesterday not to go near him. Why can you?"

"Mary, we need to get more info. I'm much better trained for this. It's simply a fact. Plus, I think you need at least one stress-free day, don't you think? I know I do after all we just talked about."

She gazed into his eyes. "Please be careful. I don't want to lose you."

"Don't worry," he chuckled. "Nobody's going to get lost."

Mary wrapped her arm around his as they left the building and headed toward the parking garage. She leaned her head against his arm and whispered, "I love you."

Bob put his arm around Mary as they walked toward the car.

Damn. This is getting awkward. She's really starting to grow on me. This is going to be tougher than I thought. The general was right. Posing as a gay couple with another male officer would have been easier.

WEDNESDAY,
9:07 AM MDT

"Stark!"

Doctor Leslie Stafford's voice bellowed as she marched into the pathology lab. The two lab technicians visibly shuddered and nearly cringed as she stomped past them. Her high heels hammered at the white speckled tile flooring. She stopped and scanned the room. There he was. She spotted the top of his head.

He was sitting behind a large bench-mounted blood chemistry analyzer. His dark scruffy hair barely poked above the analyzer's matte white and brushed aluminum cabinet. From a distance it appeared like someone left a bad toupee lying on top of the equipment.

She stomped up to him and pushed her smart phone into his face. "What's this?" she demanded.

"Oooh, cool!" he responded. "You've got one of the new Samsung Galaxy S7 phones. And the case cover matches your shoes. Tres chic," he grinned. "I bet you have a drawer full of them in different colors."

Stafford glared back. "Get serious, Stark!"

Stark pushed his eyeglasses partway down his nose and peered at the five and a half inch screen of the Samsung Galaxy. The crisp image displayed a page from Amazon's book department. "Looks like a book." He pushed his glasses back into position and smiled.

Keeping the phone's display in Stark's face, Stafford repeatedly jammed the forefinger of her free hand against the screen, causing the image to flip and turn excitedly. "Damn right it's a book. What's the book about?"

Stark put a hand over his mouth, but his eyes betrayed the laugh he was trying to stifle. Stafford could feel her blood beginning to boil.

"It's some lame-ass story about the military cloning Neanderthals for warfare," she hissed. "You've been playing me all along. Did you send that couple to my office today?"

"What couple?"

"James and Linda Williams."

"I have no idea what or who you're talking about."

"What about Birchwood? Colonel Birchwood? Did you get one of your buddies to dress-up in a rented military uniform Monday afternoon to play with my head in the maternity ward?"

At the mention of the Colonel's name, Stark's smirk disappeared. "Birchwood was here?"

"Of course he was here, you idiot. You sent him here."

"Wait. I didn't do that. I swear."

"Don't play dumb with me, Stark. I know you have a reputation for mischief. I don't understand why you're targeting me."

"I swear. I'm not making up anything."

She shoved the smart phone up to his face again. "Then what about this? How do you explain this? You read this book then thought it might be funny to use it to get under my skin. Have a little fun at my expense." She lowered the phone and leaned in toward him. "I don't appreciate it. A woman is dead and her baby is homeless right now. What kind of monster are you?"

Stark waved his hands. "Wait, please. You said Birchwood was here?"

Stafford calmed herself. "Yeah."

Stark leaped off his stool and started pacing. He passed his fingers through his hair repeatedly as he talked at the floor. "This is bad. This is bad. Blake was right."

"What the hell are you talking about? Who's Blake?"

"Blake Farnsworth. Remember the other day? You came here looking for your lab reports?"

"Yeah, it was you and Sanders."

"He had walked in on me having a phone conversation with Blake. I was telling him about the baby. He freaked. He said the military was going to come here looking for it." Stark started pacing again. "Shit, shit."

Stafford pointed a finger back at the lab's entrance. "Are you talking about the same Blake Farnsworth whose name is over the door? The rich playboy who donated a pile of money to build this new pathology lab?"

"Yeah, that's him."

Stafford was incredulous. "You know him?"

"Yes. We're friends. Like I was trying to explain to you, I was telling him about the baby."

Stafford stepped into Stark's path. "What the hell is going on here, Stark?' Her glare tore into his face. "I want some answers. Now!"

Stark cringed at her shriek. Stafford realized that the tone of her voice had become unprofessional. She glanced around the lab. The two lab technicians ducked their noses back down into their work. "Smart move," she muttered, then returned her attention to Stark. She drew one of those cleansing breaths that she had read about in some women's magazine, crossed her arms, and spoke in a steady, modulated tone. "Start talking."

"You said that Birchwood was here?" Stark asked.

Stafford crossed her arms. "Yes."

Stark's face had a questioning look. "And...?" The palms of his hands were getting sweaty. He rubbed them through his hair, which only gave it more of a bad toupee look.

Stafford gritted her teeth. "And what? You know why he was here. You sent him."

"Wait. No. I didn't send him. I never met the guy. From what I've heard about him, I don't want to." Stark paused. "Did you talk to him? What did he say?"

"He asked about Julie and the baby."

"That's all?"

"Yes. That's all."

"He didn't try to take the baby?"

"No. Of course not." She paused. "Wait. He did mention having a military family adopt it."

As if a light bulb went off in his head, Stark shouted, "Right! The fake military family. You said there was a married couple here today?"

"James and Linda Williams. They claimed to be the child's biological parents."

"You mean Robert Gordon and Mary Sullivan?"

"No. I mean James and Linda Williams. Who the hell are Robert Gordon and Mary Sullivan?"

Stark snapped his fingers. "Of course! They're only pretending to be a married couple. That makes sense."

Stafford shook her head. "Nothing you're saying is making sense."

"How did you find the book?"

Stafford's voice began to rise. "Why are you asking me all this? You set it all up. After they left my office, I tried Googling them. Nothing came up. Like they didn't even exist. Then, when I Googled Birchwood and Neanderthal together, I found this book." She waved her phone at him.

"Of course you did. The guy who wrote the book didn't change any of the names."

"Huh?"

"The writer, the author. He got a hold of classified information and leaked it as a novel. It ended up causing the mission to be scrubbed and that company to be raided. Remember the news reports last year about the law firm that was involved with human trafficking? You really think that a prestigious law firm like F&G would be selling stolen babies? It was a cover story. That firm was a front for a clandestine biotech project. They're not going to tell the public what really happened." He pointed at her phone. "This is what really happened."

Stafford put up a hand. "Wait. You're trying to convince me that this is all real?" She pointed to her smart phone. "This is true?"

"The timing is about right. The feds raided F&G about nine months ago. The baby was born this week." He waved a hand as if trying to prompt Stafford to remember some fact or detail. "Nine months?"

Stafford pressed a hand against her forehead and closed her eyes. "I can't believe I'm listening to this nutty conspiracy theory nonsense." She heard Stark talking again.

Stafford opened her eyes. Stark was waving at her to follow him.

"Let me show you something," he said.

She followed him. The two lab technicians hunched closer to their workbench as Stafford passed by.

Stark led Stafford to his desk, where he poked at his laptop. The screen displayed a DNA analysis report.

Stafford stared at the report. "I'm not a geneticist."

"I'm sure you have enough medical training to understand," he grinned. "I'll walk you through it."

Stafford listened as Stark explained. She noticed how serious his tone had become; almost professorial. He scrolled the multipage report up and down the screen, pointing his fingers at tables and charts. Then he brought up a few other reports and graphics and displayed them side by side with the first, pointing out their similarities and differences. Finally, he leaned back against the desk and looked at her.

Stafford studied the screen. Without looking up, she said, "I don't believe what I'm seeing."

"Believe it."

Stafford pondered for a moment. "That does explain the diet change, and the sclera." She shook her head. "Still, it seems too farfetched."

Stark looked right at her. His expression was unusually serious. "Do your own DNA analysis."

"This is a lot of work," Stafford replied. "I can't believe that even you would go through this much effort for a practical joke."

"You said the baby was okay?"

"Yeah, we stabilized the infant. Upped her protein and fat intake. She's doing fine now and is out of the NICU." She paused, then asked, "What about the extra-long cord?"

"Yeah…" He scratched at his beard and shrugged. "No explanation for that."

The two doctors stood silently, staring at the laptop display. The only sounds were the ventilation system and the occasional beeps, whirs, and clicks from equipment that the two lab technicians were operating. Stafford drew a breath. Without looking up, she asked, "So what killed Julie?"

"It was a mistake," Stark responded. "I believe it was supposed to kill the baby. It was probably supposed to be a fail-safe so that if Julie or the other surrogates skipped out, their unborn children would be stillborn. The military couldn't have live Neanderthals getting into civilian hands. Whatever the fail-safe was, it didn't work. Or I should say it worked the wrong way; killing the mother and leaving the child alive. That's why Birchwood's trying to get the baby. That's why Robert and Mary are here. What I don't understand is why they're not working together."

Stafford looked up at Stark. "That couple seemed really apprehensive about Birchwood, almost frightened."

"They should be."

"Why's that?"

Stark became animated again. "He's nuts." Stark tried to step away but was boxed in between Stafford and his desk. She gave him some space. He walked in a tight circle as he spoke. "Blake filled me in about him. Birchwood's suffering from PTSD. And he lost his younger brother in Afghanistan. That pushed him over the edge. There's no telling what he's up to or what he wants to do with the baby."

"You're saying that the child is in danger?"

Stark became visibly agitated. "Yes. Yes."

"What about this Farnsworth guy?" she asked. "Can he help? Where is he?"

Stark still seemed a bit distracted. "I wish I knew. He said he was coming right here. I tried calling but I got no answer."

"Birchwood?" she uttered, but then caught herself and shook her head. "Damn! Now you got me believing in your conspiracy."

The old Stark that she knew seemed to be back. "No, I don't think Birchwood got to him. Blake's got a lot of bucks and connections. I'm sure that he's okay. I'll bet he's gotten distracted by some young lady."

"You think that Robert and Mary aren't working with Birchwood?" Stafford asked.

"Not anymore," he replied. "It's hard to believe that they would have come here like that. Alone. With no leverage to take the baby."

"I need to go talk to someone." Stafford pointed and twirled a finger back in the direction of where she first found him in the lab. "You keep working." She turned on her heel and walked toward the lab door.

Stark called after her, "So, this was like our first date, right?"

She smirked and waved back at him as she left the lab. "In your dreams, Stark."

WEDNESDAY,
9:29 AM MDT

Doctor Stafford stood at the office suite door, one hand on the handle, reading the engraved eye-level nameplate. It read DR. ERIC PATTERSON, O.D. ORTHOPEDICS. She let go and turned away, ready to head back to her office.

This is nuts. It can't be true. I saw the data. Why would he be making up such a preposterous story?

She turned around and reached for the door handle, drew a breath, opened the door, and stepped inside. The beige-walled office was barely appointed with furniture and fixtures from a commercial supply house. Artwork unworthy for motel rooms hung on the walls. A handful of the waiting room chairs held patients with crutches, casts, and foot braces. The receptionist looked up from behind a sliding glass partition bordered by tattered handouts and flyers. "Oh. Doctor Stafford. Um, I don't believe he's expecting you."

Stafford nodded toward Patterson's inner office. Its door was closed. "Is he with a patient?"

"He's about to see one." The receptionist raised a hand. "No. Wait. You can't go in there."

It was too late. Stafford had already marched over to Eric's office, opened the door and walked in. Patterson was sitting behind a small metal desk that had seen better days. He wore a rumpled white lab coat, his tie was loosened and the top button of his blue button-down shirt was undone.

"I need to talk," she announced.

Patterson closed the lid of his laptop and tossed his reading glasses on his desk. "You can't simply barge into my office during office hours. I have patients to see."

"I said, we need to talk."

"Leslie. Now is not the time or the place to discuss what happened between us yesterday."

"I don't want to talk about that."

Patterson crossed his arms and leaned back in his chair. A metallic squeak prefaced his statement. "Well, then what's so important that you come crashing into my office?"

"I just came from the pathology lab. I know what killed Julie. I think Stark really did discover a Neanderthal infant."

"Stark? Doctor Daniel Stark? That loony pathologist? What crazy conspiracy theory is he spouting now?"

"I've seen his data. The genome reports. The DNA analysis."

Patterson spread his arms. "Leslie, I have no idea what you're talking about."

"Remember our conversation in my office a couple of days ago?"

"How could I forget it? I learned what a greedy, manipulative narcissist you really are."

"That's not fair!"

He leaned forward, resting his arms on the desk. "It's quite fair. You told me how you were pimping out young women's wombs as surrogates."

Stafford waved her hands. "Please, Eric. Stop. That's not what I'm here about."

Another metallic squeak punctuated the conversation as Patterson reclined. "I'm listening."

"Remember how I told you about Julie, the surrogate that died during childbirth."

"How could I forget? That's when the truth about you starting coming out."

"Please, stop being judgmental and listen to me."

"I remember the conversation, Leslie. You told me the story about Julie, her difficult pregnancy, her traumatic death. The poor girl didn't deserve any of that. What? Are you feeling guilty now?"

"What else did I tell you?"

"I don't know. You mentioned that you were waiting for labs results. Yes, you got a phone call from pathology saying that the autopsy was delayed."

"And…."

"And what? Leslie, I don't have time for games." He moved to stand. She raised a hand again to stop him. Patterson eased back into his seat.

"Think. What else did I say? Who did I say came to the maternity ward to see Julie's baby?"

"Oh, yeah. The soldier with the southern accent."

"Right, exactly."

"So?"

"It's all real."

"What's real?"

"That baby. The infant that Julie was carrying. It's a real live Neanderthal."

"Leslie, do you realize what you're saying?"

"Yeah, it's incredible, isn't it?"

"Have you gone insane?"

"No, I haven't. Stark fit all the pieces together for me. There's a secret government project to clone Neanderthals to use as soldiers. Julie must have been recruited without her knowledge to carry one of the clones."

"Are you hearing what's coming out of your mouth? You're standing here, in my office, as a board certified obstetrician, and telling me that your deceased patient gave birth to an extinct species of humans."

Stafford opened her mouth to speak, then stopped.

What the hell am I talking about?

"It does sound crazy, doesn't it?" she admitted.

"Think about it, Leslie. Cloning technology has progressed rapidly, but cloning an extinct species? That's farfetched. No one's ever successfully cloned any extinct mammal, let alone an extinct species of human. You think a surrogate for hire, one you knew personally, actually carried a cloned Neanderthal to term and gave birth to it? It's ludicrous. Science fiction. Who would have chosen Julie to be the surrogate? How would they have impregnated here? Why would she be free, roaming around, with what would be the most valuable fetus in the world inside of her?"

He's right. How the hell did Stark convince me of his deranged theory?

"That's what I thought, too. In fact, that's what I had been thinking all along while Stark was trying to convince me about his Neanderthal theories. I figured that he didn't know what he was talking about, or flubbed/botched the DNA sequencing, or something. But then he showed me all this data, DNA analysis of the infant, articles about Neanderthal genome research."

"DNA analysis that only he did? Articles posted on the internet? Did he show you anything that was peer reviewed and published? Come on, Leslie. Regardless of what I said about you a few minutes ago, you are the most pragmatic, logical physician that I know. How could you fall for Stark's gibberish?"

Patterson shifted in his seat, causing its reclining mechanism to croak. "The guy's a little nutty if you ask me. I've never had to deal with him directly. But from what I hear.... Well.... I don't want to say anything rude, but I don't know how he even got the lab position that he has. Senior Pathologist? Please! The guy used to work in a morgue."

Stafford put her hand to her head and closed her eyes. She thought back to her conversation with Stark. "There's this book that he talked about. A book that he says describes the secret government project."

Patterson reached into a desk drawer and withdrew a paperback book. The cover was the same as Stafford had seen earlier that day on Amazon. "Are you talking about this book?"

Her eyes grew wide. "Wait! When did you get that? You already know about this?" Stafford's voice grew tense. "Did you already talk to Stark?"

"No. Of course not. Why the hell would I have a conversation with him?"

"Then why do you have a copy of that book?"

"I like to read sci-fi. You'd know that if you actually listened to me when I talk rather than treating me like your dress-up Ken doll. This book caught my eye because the story is set right here in South Dakota. Stark probably read it, too, and got sucked into a fantasy spun by the author. He's like one of those dungeon and dragon fanatics who get so immersed in the game that they begin to blur reality with their fictional world."

"I feel like an idiot."

"Look, Leslie. I know you've had a really rough week, with Julie dying and all. But I also can't forget the conversation we had yesterday. It really made me think."

He checked his watch. "I've got a patient waiting. Can we deal with all this later, when we can both sit down and really talk it out?" Patterson stood, walked to his office door and opened it. "Get some rest, Leslie. You look like you need it."

Stafford plodded out of Patterson's office and down the hall toward the elevator. In her mind she replayed the conversation she had with Stark earlier that morning. She remembered that he exhibited some strange symptoms. They seemed to her like a mild epileptic seizure.

Maybe he has a brain tumor? Or maybe something neurological that's affecting his judgment? Maybe that's what's making him believe in these conspiracy theories?

Stafford's smartphone chirped and vibrated. She pulled it from her pocket and swiped its screen. "Stafford here."

"Doctor Stafford. You're needed in maternity, stat. There's an emergency C-section."

Stafford ripped off her high heels and broke into a run. "I'm on my way," she barked and headed for the stairwell.

WEDNESDAY,
8:12 PM MDT

Blake Farnsworth savored his tequila sunset. He preferred the refreshing sunset over its more syrupy sweet kin. It also reminded him that all good things come to an end, and enjoying the journey was paramount.

The brim of his Montecristi panama was tipped down to shield his eyes from the setting sun. From his vantage point at one of the bistro's outdoor tables, Farnsworth was able to survey quite a bit of Rapid City's Downtown Square. The city's Main Street Square featured live concerts, art shows, and other cultural events. He didn't need to be elsewhere.

People couldn't understand why he stuck around after the raid on his grandfather's firm. Released from his obligations at the company, and flush with cash, there seemed to be little else holding him here. Farnsworth thought otherwise. As he surveyed the square full of smiling faces, steady commerce, and pleasant summer weather, he felt that there was nowhere else to start a fresh new journey. And he had plans.

He caught sight of his friend, Doctor Daniel Stark, making his way through the ambling tourists toward the cluster of petite bistro tables. Farnsworth thought he could spot the scientist approaching from a mile away; the man has such a characteristic gait. Not quite a swagger. More like an animated shuffle. Farnsworth couldn't help but smile.

There was something infectious about Stark. Something that brought out the child in people. He was a refreshing change from the stiff suited automatons that Farnsworth had been forced to interact with when he had worked at F&G.

"Hey! Blake. You made it here before me." Stark waved and hollered as he approached.

Farnsworth noted that Stark could never wait to reach the table before putting his mouth in motion. The man was a born talker.

Farnsworth didn't bother rising to greet Stark as he finished traversing those last few steps. "Hey, Daniel," he called back, drink in hand. "I jumped into my plane and headed here right after our conversation. Hey, how's the new job working out so far?" Farnsworth winked. "Do you like your new boss?"

"How did you get both of us working together? And at the hospital's new pathology lab? You must have some serious connections."

Farnsworth took another sip of his drink. "Only the best that money can buy. It helps when one donates the money to build a new pathology lab." He raised an arm and a young waitress scurried over to the table carrying a cappuccino.

Stark always ordered a cappuccino, Farnsworth had noted, and he had preordered for his friend. Farnsworth didn't have the heart to tell Stark that it wasn't an afternoon beverage. Instead, he enjoyed watching Stark inspect and analyze the drink's stiff foam topping, prodding at it with his spoon and watching with amazement how much sugar could be made to rest on the bed of foam before it collapsed like a sinkhole swallowing a snowfield.

Farnsworth pulled Stark's attention away from the frothy beverage. "Tell me more about this infant," he asked.

Stark's eyes lit up. Still grasping his spoon, he began speaking. The spoon moved to and fro as he spoke; the last bits foam that had clung to it flying into the air. "It's incredible. I couldn't believe the data. I ran the samples two and three times to be sure."

"And what did you find?"

"The correlation to known Neanderthal DNA was nearly ninety-two percent!" Stark's spoon danced in the air as he spoke. "Ninety-two percent. It's like a time machine deposited a newborn Neanderthal right here in this city."

"Does anyone else know about this?"

"Well, I told Sanders, but he didn't listen. He never listens. Sometimes I think that when I talk about this, all he hears is 'blah blah, Neanderthal, blah blah'. He has no idea what he's missing."

"Anyone else?"

"Yeah, I told Doctor Leslie Stafford. She's the doctor who had the specimens sent to the lab and ordered all the tests. At first I wasn't sure if she suspected anything weird or if she was only following protocol. I held on to the autopsy report and the DNA analysis. She came looking for it yesterday when I was talking to you on the phone while you were on your ski trip. Hey, how was that trip? Did you actually jump out of a helicopter with skis strapped to your feet? You are a crazy dude, you know that?"

"I cut the trip short right after our conversation. I wanted to get here as soon as possible so that I could talk to you in person."

"Wow. I didn't think that you were all that interested in Neanderthals or paleo-genetics."

"It's a budding interest. And I enjoy listening to you talk about it. You're right about Sanders. He doesn't know what he's missing."

This put a broad smile on Stark's face and he proceeded to regale Farnsworth with all the possibilities of how this unique infant came to be. "It couldn't have happened naturally, spontaneously," he said. "The odds of a lineage of disparate DNA from an ancestral lineage converging to produce such a highly concentrated occurrence of pure Neanderthal genetic material are infinitesimal. It had to be manipulated artificially." He leaned in. "It's one of the ones that F&G created, isn't it?"

"Yes. And there may be others."

Stark tossed his spoon on the table. "No way! More than one living Neanderthal?" He rubbed his hands together. "This is so exciting."

Farnsworth glanced around at the other patrons. They all seemed uninterested in the conversation. "Calm down, Daniel. Someone's going to come looking for these babies and they may not be interested in the scientific aspects. They may be more interested in what the babies are worth on the black market or to the military. You can't tell anyone about this child."

"What about Doctor Stafford? She already knows. I told her and I think she might actually believe me."

"Is she doing anything about it? Did she tell the hospital administration?"

"Not that I know of. I'm not sure I convinced her. And I don't think she's all that interested even though she listened to me, unlike Sanders. She's more interested in her clothes and shoes." He shook his head.

"So no one else has come to you asking for the results of all your tests?"

Stark shook his head. "No."

"Good." Farnsworth paused. "What about Stafford? Did she say if anyone came to her or talked to her about this?"

"Yeah, as a matter of fact. She told me that a married couple came to her claiming that they were the child's biological parents. They told her that the woman who gave birth and then died was a surrogate carrying their child."

Farnsworth paused and thought.

Must have been Gordon and Sullivan. The military must be looking for this baby.

He continued to quiz his friend. "Are those the only two people who spoke with Stafford?

"No, she said that a Colonel Birchwood was there, too."

"Birchwood? He was with the couple?"

"No, Doctor Stafford said he was at the hospital the day before. He was in the maternity ward."

Shit. Birchwood is alive and looking for the child.

Farnsworth pressed Stark for more details. "From what Stafford told you, did it seem like the couple and the Colonel were working together?"

Farnsworth could see that Stark was searching through his mind. Daniel shook his head. "No, I don't think they are working together. Doctor Stafford said something about the couple not being happy when she told them about Colonel Birchwood."

Farnsworth thought about the possibilities.

Why wouldn't they be working together? Now I'm wondering which of them, if any, are still working with General Holbrooke. If Birchwood is acting alone, what's his agenda? What would he want with the infant?

Then again, what would Gordon and Sullivan want with the infant if they're not retrieving it for the military? None of this is making any sense.

If the military wanted this child, they could simply claim guardianship of it, especially since the mother is dead and no relatives are stepping forward. They could easily concoct a scenario to support their taking custody of the child.

"Think, Daniel. What else did Stafford say about the couple or about Birchwood? Did she say anything about custody of the child?"

Again, Farnsworth remained quiet as Stark searched through what must have been a mountain of facts and trivia stored inside his head. "Yes! I remember. She said something about a military family that was going to be foster parents for it."

"Who said this? Birchwood or the couple?" Farnsworth asked.

"It was Colonel Birchwood. Doctor Stafford said that Colonel Birchwood told her that a military family was going to adopt it."

"Did he say who the family was? Did Birchwood tell Stafford that the couple was the military family?"

Stark shook his head. "I don't think so. I'm not sure. Sorry. I got so nervous when she told me about Colonel Birchwood being in the same hospital where I work. I read about him in the book. If he's really like that in person…." His voice trailed off.

"Don't worry about Birchwood. I'm certain that he doesn't know anything about you."

Stark squirmed in his seat. His voice was flustered. "But he knows about Leslie."

Farnsworth paused. He looked at the worry in Stark's face. He leaned back. "You have a thing for Stafford, don't you?"

Stark blushed. "No, no," he stammered. "Well, maybe a little. I like the way she dresses." He smiled.

"I don't think Birchwood is interested in Stafford. He wants the baby. As long as Stafford stays out of his way, she'll be fine. Besides, I think Doctor Stafford is quite able to take care of herself."

"What makes you think that?"

Farnsworth leaned forward. "Daniel. My friend. Women like Stafford dress that way for one reason; to take advantage of people; people like you and me, and Doctor Patterson, and Sanders. We get mesmerized by the glamour and fancy clothes, and before we know it, we're under their spell. That's what happened to Julie. I wouldn't be surprised if Stafford was actually in on the whole thing with F&G or the military. Think about it. She had the contacts with her profession. F&G probably came to her looking for surrogates. She's trying to throw you off to keep you from finding the truth."

"You think so?"

"Yes. And I think the more you poke around, the more complicated it's going to become."

"But I really want to study the Neanderthal."

"Daniel. Stop and think. It's you against the military. Who do you think is going to win?"

Stark sat and stared at his cold cappuccino. The froth had dissipated leaving only a latte colored liquid. "What if I went to work for them?" he blurted out. "What if I became a consultant for them? I do know a lot about the genetics of Neanderthals." His face came alive. "I'm practically an expert."

"Daniel. I really don't want to burst your bubble but the military is not going to want you. I'm sure they already have their experts. They did know enough to create this baby."

Farnsworth paused and watched the smile fade from Stark's eyes. "Here's what I would do. Get all the data and specimens that you can, as soon as you can. Put them in a safe place in your lab, away from Sanders and the lab techs. Then you can perform your own research independently."

"But I'll be working alone and I won't have all the facilities that I bet the military has."

"You'll have the hospital's new pathology lab. You've got the latest cutting edge equipment, thanks to me. It'll be *your* research. You'll be in control. You'll decide what direction it will take." Farnsworth paused. "If you were working as a consultant for the military you would have to do what they tell you. All the time. It wouldn't be like working for Sanders."

Farnsworth could see that Stark was coming around to this line of thought. "And whatever you do, whatever you discover, it'll be all yours. You'll be able to publish freely. People will know your name. Hell, you'll make it to the cover of Scientific American. You won't get any of that in the military. You'll just be another lab rat running tests and writing reports."

"What about Leslie, I mean Doctor Stafford? She knows about all this. I told her."

"Think about how she's treated you up to now. Especially with all the Neanderthal related discoveries you've made over the past year. She might be jealous. She had this data staring her in the face and they didn't even see it. She actually had access to the Neanderthal baby before it was even born."

"But, she didn't know it was Neanderthal then."

"Doesn't matter. What matters is how she treated you and what she thought of your ideas afterwards. She knew that there was a problem with the pregnancy and she ignored the data. If she had paid attention and had done the right tests, she would be the one to soon become famous, not you. But it's you, the scientist with the open mind, who is deserving of this discovery. You earned it."

"How am I supposed to keep her from the using the data? They're hospital records now. And there are laws about medical record privacy."

"I read the HIPAA regulations. There are contingencies for medical research. Exactly for the type of research that you are going to pursue. Since Julie is dead, the regulations permit use of her medical data for scientific research. All you have to do is announce your research to the hospital administration. And do it before Stafford does."

"What about the infant's medical records?"

"Daniel, the HIPAA laws cover humans, not Neanderthals. You can do whatever you want with that data and the specimens."

Stark's eyes grew wide. Farnsworth saw that he had Stark won over.

This worked perfectly. Regardless of what happened to the infant, regardless of whether or not Birchwood and the Gordons were working together, he would at least have enough data to restart a project in a newly formed private research firm. The monetary potential was incalculable.

He watched Stark. The scientist had rested his chin in a hand and his eyes were gazing up and off into the distance. Farnsworth was certain that he had recruited the lead scientist for his new firm; hook, line and sinker.

WEDNESDAY,
10:43 PM MDT

With her arms wrapped around Bob's neck and her eyes locked on his, Mary eased back into the plush sofa cushions in the dimly lit living room. She hugged his muscular frame tightly, relishing the feel of his hard chest against her bare breasts.

Light from images flickering across the nearby TV screen danced across her face. She closed her eyes and tuned-out the saccharine dialogue from the made-for-TV romance. It had done its job getting her into the mood. Now if she could only stay in it.

Mary gasped then moaned softly as Bob slowly made his way into her. She slid her hands down the small of his back, spread her fingers around his firm ass and pushed him deeper. Neurotransmitters flooded the pleasure centers of her brain, forcing away all other thoughts and sounds. She could feel her breaths quicken and a warm rush enveloped her.

The urgent voice of a newscaster seeped into Mary's consciousness. "…Greyhound bus accident has sent scores of injured passengers to the E.R." reported the newscaster. "No word yet on the …"

Mary ignored the voice. She wasn't going to let anything interrupt the bliss she was experiencing. She could tell that Bob felt the same way as one of his gentle hands lifted away from her skin and groped around for the TV remote.

"Don't worry about it," she breathed into his ear. "I can tune it out."

"I'm not taking any chances," he whispered. "I know how your brain works."

Mary ignored his tease. Yes, it was true that any random word or phrase could send her mind into a cascade of hyper-associativity. It was a valuable asset when analyzing complex legal issues. It was more than unwelcome when she simply wanted to abandon herself to primal instincts.

"Please, don't stop," she murmured.

Bob's hand returned to cupping her breast.

The newscaster's voice droned in the background.

…*flood of casualties*…

Snippets of his reporting wriggled through the filters in Mary's mind.

… *E.R. and hospital staff overwhelmed*…

One phrase landed on a certain synapse, which fired and awoke another clump of neurons deep within the prefrontal cortex. More neurons fired, waking Mary's cerebral cortex. Thoughts formed. They fought their way through her brain's dopamine drenched pleasure centers fueling the primal emotions that kept their bodies interlocked. The thoughts coalesced into theories about cause and effect; consequences of actions; distractions and subterfuge.

"He's taking it. Tonight!" Mary's body bolted upright, flinging Bob off the couch and onto the floor.

"Huh? What?" Bob shook his head, pushed himself off the carpet, yanked up his pants and crawled back up onto the sofa.

"Birchwood!" He's stealing the baby! Tonight. Right now!"

Bob shook his head and stared back. Mary grabbed his arm and pointed to the TV which was still showing the special news report that had interrupted the movie. An aerial view of the calamity filled the screen. Spotlights from a helicopter played along the overpass connecting interstate I-90 to the I-190 connecter. A mangled coach bus lay on its side below the overpass's torn guardrails.

"Mary. Calm down. What are you all excited about? What's this about Birchwood and the baby?"

"He's stealing it right now!" Mary's outstretched arm waved and pointed. "Can't you see?"

Bob looked over at the TV then back to Mary. "There's a bus accident. What's this have to do with Birchwood or the baby? It's safe. It's in the hospital."

"Ugh!" Mary grabbed Bob's arm. "Don't you see? Birchwood did that!" She pointed back at the TV. "We need to go there. Now!"

"Mary, I'm not taking you anywhere until you calm down and explain to me what's going through your head."

Mary drew a breath. A deep, cleansing breath. She closed her eyes and slowly let the air out of her lungs. Another cleansing breath. Slow release. One more.

She opened her eyes. Bob was watching her; his eyes wide; his expression expectant. She spoke in low, steady tones. "Birchwood did something to force that bus off the highway. He knows the accident will send dozens of casualties to the hospital. He's creating a distraction by flooding the E.R. with all those injured people. The hospital staff will be overwhelmed. Nurses will be drawn from other departments, like the maternity ward, to assist. With all the commotion, nobody will be watching the infants."

She stopped explaining and looked at Bob's eyes.

He stood. "Get dressed," he ordered. "Grab the bags. I'll get the car. We're heading to the hospital."

WEDNESDAY,
11:13 PM MDT

Colonel Birchwood picked and dodged his way through the commotion in the hospital E.R.

The driver of a Greyhound bus had lost control and the vehicle had careened off a highway overpass. The injured flooded the E.R. where a triage station was set up. It was all hands on deck for the hospital staff, leaving many other departments, including the maternity ward, understaffed.

Police officers, paramedics, and EMTs jostled around each other and the medical staff, each person trying to do his or her job of saving the injured while also finding answers for the cause of the calamity.

Passengers had reported hearing gunshots immediately before the accident. Investigators discovered bullet holes in the vehicle's tires. Fearing a possible terrorist attack, the FBI and homeland security were called in. At a time like this, no one was going to question a person wearing a military uniform. The Colonel had no problem blending into the scene.

Birchwood spotted a door marked HOSPITAL STAFF ONLY. He strode toward it, swung open the door, and kept moving. His eyes darted about, checking for security cameras and hospital staff. He proceeded down an empty corridor, past radiology, to a stairwell. A quick jaunt up four flights of stairs and he was in the maternity ward.

The lights were dimmed. The hallway was empty. The nurse's station was at the other end. Between him and the station, halfway down the hall, was the nursery. Its glass viewing windows reflected the soft corridor lighting.

A few short days ago Birchwood stood at those windows planning his moves; biding his time; watching the patterns of the staff; memorizing faces; and names. Now the plan was in motion.

He recognized Nurse Jackson sitting alone at the nurse's station, her gaze fixed on a computer display. As he expected, the younger nurses had gone to the E.R. to deal with the incoming casualties. The older, overweight nurse served his plans nicely. Unless some alarm went off, she would most likely stay planted in her seat.

Birchwood stole quietly down the corridor and slipped into the sparsely populated nursery. The handful of infants were all sleeping soundly. The subdued lighting reassured him that any security cameras would have a difficult time grabbing his image.

He walked past each bassinet, inspecting the nametags. Most were empty and untagged. Other bassinets were tagged but unoccupied; their residents most likely nursing or sleeping with the mother.

He came to the last bassinet in the row. The tag read '*Baby Jane Doe*'. Birchwood examined the sleeping infant's features closely; red hair, the blend of Caucasian and Asian facial features, large eye sockets. This infant was the target to be acquired.

He reached into a pocket and retrieved a small syringe. He uncapped it, reached into the bassinet, and thrust the needle into the upper thigh of the sleeping child. Its eyes flew open then scrunched shut. Its mouth opened in a grimace, but no sound emerged. The face stayed frozen in a look of surprise.

Birchwood capped and slipped the spent syringe back into his pocket then reached in to scoop the paralyzed child into his arms.

The overhead lights flared on.

"Who the hell are you and what the hell are you doing in my nursery?" a female voice bellowed from behind.

Birchwood spun around.

The tall, husky figure of Nurse Jackson stood in the doorway. With her arms akimbo and feet planted in a wide stance, her burly body fully blocked the nearest exit. Her large feet were encased in blocky white footwear that was planted solidly at the lower end of what could only be described as cankles. Her eyes glared from behind an ornate set of horned-rimmed glasses.

"Put down that baby. Now!" she barked as she reached for the wall phone, her immense figure blocking Birchwood's escape route.

Birchwood scooped up the paralyzed child, blankets and all, and stormed toward the exit. He cradled the infant in one arm, like a football. With the other hand he reached out and ripped the phone handset from Jackson's ear. He wrapped the cord once around her neck and kept moving, still gripping the handset.

The staggering nurse gasped and clawed at the cord tightening around her neck like a garrote.

Birchwood kept moving, cradling the infant and gripping the phone cord and handset. The cord stretched taut behind him. He released his grip on the handset and cord only after hearing the thud of a falling body, followed by the clattering of the phone that had been ripped from the wall by the dead weight of the now unconscious nurse.

The few sleeping infants had been startled awake by the lights and bellowing and were wailing. The ruckus had also drawn a few weary mothers and disheveled dads from within the rooms along Birchwood's escape route.

Cradling the paralyzed, soundless infant like a football, Birchwood charged through the gauntlet of staggering, half-awake parents and headed toward the stairwell like a power runningback with the goal line in sight.

He hustled down the four flights of stairs, then cut to the left, toward the main entrance; the opposite direction from the E.R. His earlier recon had indicated that at this time of night, the main lobby would be deserted. He did not want to force his way through a moving crowd of crutches, wheelchairs and gurneys back at the E.R.

Part way across the empty main lobby Birchwood spied a uniformed figure bolt from behind an information kiosk. It was Captain Robert Gordon.

Without breaking his stride, Birchwood feigned to the right then darted to the left, but Captain Gordon shadowed him like a defensive linebacker.

"What are you doing soldier?" Birchwood demanded as he found himself forced into a corner away from the lobby's main doors.

"Are you responsible for this?" Gordon's arms were outstretched, one flailing toward the general direction of the E.R., the other jabbing at Birchwood.

"It was necessary." Birchwood's eyes darted back and forth, looking for an escape.

"Have you gone completely mad? You fired on a busload of civilians? You risked all those innocent lives to create a diversion so you could steal this child?"

The Colonel shuffled and feigned. "No one must discover the existence of this child."

Gordon worked him deeper into the corner. "What did you do to it? It's not crying." He glared at Birchwood. "It's not making any sounds at all! You didn't kill it, did you?"

"Fast acting paralysis on the voluntary nervous system. Autonomic nervous system is still functioning normally. It will survive."

Gordon's lips curled. "It better. I can't believe you did this to a child."

Birchwood glanced around, looking for a way to slip past his adversary. Gordon had him pinned between an information kiosk and an ATM. His back against the kiosk, the only escape was to barrel through his opponent. He wrapped his arms around his prize, lowered a shoulder toward Gordon, and made his move.

A quick sting in the back of his neck stopped his motion almost before it started. He instinctively reached back as if to slap a mosquito. His right arm froze halfway up.

A female voice whispered into his ear. "Yeah, I know about the fast-acting paralysis, too."

The voice belonged to Lieutenant Mary Sullivan. He could feel her hot breath on the nape of his neck.

"How's it feel?" she hissed. "Now you know what this poor child is going through."

Birchwood tried to speak, but his lips and jaw were immobile. A stream of modulated hissing sounds emerged from his open mouth, sounding like someone muttering in their sleep. Frozen muscles robbed him of the fine motor control required to keep his balance and remain standing. He toppled like a statue unanchored from its pedestal.

Mary snatched the infant from his arms as he fell.

No one tried to catch the Colonel.

He hit the marble floor hard; face down, the outstretched elbow of his right arm taking the brunt of the fall and pitching him over onto his back.

Not being able to move his head or even his eyeballs, his field of vision was locked to the ceiling above him. His mind screamed silently from the sharp, stabbing pain of a snapped forearm and dislocated shoulder.

Although his peripheral vision allowed him to see the mangled arm that was jammed against his face, it was insufficient to allow even a glimpse of his attackers. However, they could be heard quite plainly.

"Jesus! I thought he was going to bounce right back up on his feet the way he hit the floor." Gordon's voice sounded astonished, as if he had never seen a soldier fall in battle before. "How long will he be out?"

"About an hour or so before it wears off," Mary responded. "It's fast acting but also metabolizes pretty quickly, so when it does wear off, he's going to start moving pretty quick. That is, if the police don't find him first."

"Plenty of time to get some distance between us and this hospital."

Birchwood heard footsteps scuffling around, then heard Mary ask, "How's the baby?"

"It'll be okay," Gordon replied. "But it's going to be very cranky in about an hour. You packed lots of formula, right?"

"And diapers, wipes, creams, baby powder, pacifier...." Mary rattled off.

"Wow. You're really getting into this whole motherhood thing."

Mary's tone sounded defensive. "What's that supposed to mean?"

"I only meant that you're prepared, that's all."

The conversation stopped.

Footsteps approached.

Mary's face came into Birchwood's limited view. She must have been bending or kneeling over him because she got right into his face. She grinned and patted his cheek, then spat out the word, "Asshole."

"Let's move!" Gordon's voice sounded more distant. He must have already moved toward an exit.

Mary's face disappeared from view and Birchwood was left staring at the ceiling. The heel of a boot appeared above his face. It smashed down on his nose, breaking it. Birchwood's mind burst into another silent scream. Blood trickled down his cheeks.

Gordon's voice shouted in the distance. "Mary! That's enough! Let's move!"

The scuffling sounds of footsteps receded to his left, followed by the sounds of the main door crash bars engaging as the doors opened, then closed.

Birchwood was alone in the dimly lit lobby. Agonizing pain ripped through his broken arm and smashed face. Warm rivulets of blood ran down his cheeks. His mind smoldered, then flared, as it fought to scream the words through his unmoving lips.

You. Will. Pay. For. This.

WEDNESDAY, 11:36 PM MDT

Bob watched the lights of the city receding in the rear-view mirror as he drove southeast under the pastel twilight of South Dakota's Black Hills. Mary sat stone-still in the passenger seat next to him. Her face was expressionless. She hadn't said a word since they fled the hospital. He eyed her, started to say something, but stopped. He focused back on the road. After a few minutes he worked up the courage.

"Hey."

Mary did not respond.

"Mary? You okay?"

"Huh? What are you talking about?"

"Shit, Mary, you were pretty ruthless back there."

"What do you mean?"

"What you did to Birchwood once he was down."

She stared straight ahead. "He deserved it," she muttered.

"He was already subdued. There was nothing more we needed to do. He couldn't retaliate."

"I said he deserved it," she snarled. She looked back and smiled at the infant sleeping in the car seat. "Momma's gonna protect you." She turned back to Bob. "Where we heading?"

Bob was reluctant to answer. He could tell that Mary was not right.

She's traumatized. I've got to keep her calm and watch what I say…and how I say it.

"I don't know the ultimate destination. General Holbrooke gave me GPS coordinates for the navigation system. I'm, I mean we're to drive to this destination then report in."

"So you have no idea where he's having us drive to? I thought we were taking the baby to a military family who would protect and raise it."

"Yes, that's the plan."

"But you have no idea who they are or where they live?"

"The General didn't fill me in on the details, Mary."

"Why is he being so secretive? Doesn't he trust us?" Her tone was impertinent.

Bob raised an eyebrow. "Of course he trusts us. We have the child. He has to trust us."

She crossed her arms and went back to staring straight ahead. "He's not telling us where we're going."

Bob thought for a minute before speaking. "Maybe he wants to make sure we're not being followed. Maybe the route we're taking is only in his head, and his alone. He's having us drive to certain checkpoints to make sure we're not being followed, then when we report in, he gives us the coordinates for the next segment of the trip."

"Seems more risky to me."

"I'm not going to second-guess the General."

"I'm not asking you to question his orders. I'm asking you to be honest with me."

Bob watched the road unwinding ahead of him.

What's going through her head? I can't see how she would suspect anything. Damn, maybe Holbrooke was right. What have I got myself into?

He thought for a moment.

She's not used to being in the field. Maybe the encounter with Birchwood was too much for her to handle.

He glanced at her. "We have a long drive ahead of us. You should get some sleep."

"Who's going to keep you awake? And who's going to watch the baby?"

"I'll be fine, and the baby's not going anywhere, except with us. It's safe. We'll protect it."

He motioned for her to settle back and get some rest. She looked back at the infant, then at Bob, then finally reclined her seat and closed her eyes.

THURSDAY, 12:17 AM MDT

Mary jerked upright in her seat. "Do you hear that?"

"Hear what?"

"That sound."

Rob glanced in the rearview mirror. "The baby? It's sleeping."

"No, no. It's a droning sound. Like a small airplane. Shit. We're being followed!"

"We're not being followed. Birchwood is pasted to the lobby floor back at the hospital, right where you left him. Who else would know what we're up to or where we're heading?"

"We need to be sure. We need to stop and check."

"Mary. Don't you realize that if I stopped the car, if someone was flying overhead and they were really tracking us, they would see us stop? They would know that we know we're being followed. We'd give ourselves away."

"We need to protect this baby!"

"We are. We're on a deserted road, heading to a place where this baby will be safe." He checked the rearview mirror again. "There's no one following us."

"Wait! It's back again! The droning sound. Stop the car. Now."

She yanked the steering wheel from his hands. The vehicle veered onto the road's hard-scrabble shoulder and came to a stop.

"Goddamn it, Mary! What the hell are you trying to do? Kill us and the baby?"

She crossed her arms and looked away from him. "I said we're being followed."

"Fine. I'll check."

He shoved open his door and stepped into the brisk night air.

Alone in the car, Mary mumbled to herself. "We're being followed. I know we're being followed. They know. We can't stay here." She started climbing over the center console when the driver door opened and Gordon sat down behind the wheel.

"There's nothing out there. No droning. No aircraft lights, no other cars. Nothing. Just a full moon."

"So, you think I'm hearing things now?"

"No, I think you're so pumped up on adrenaline that your mind is racing, play tricks on you. Face it, Mary. You're not trained for field operative mission and maybe you're not cut out for it either. The stress is getting to you. Please, take a deep breath. Sit back. Relax. Get some shut-eye. We have a long drive and I'll need you to do some driving later."

Mary looked out her window at the moonlit prairie. She imagined her mind being as peaceful as this serene landscape. She twisted around to check on the child. It was fast asleep. She sank deeper into her seat, closed her eyes and tried to do the same.

THURSDAY,
12:17 AM MDT

Red is grey, and yellow, white.

The lyrics from The Moody Blues, 'Days of Future Passed' album, echoed in Farnsworth's mind as he piloted his single engine Cessna 172S Skyhawk low over the moonlit prairie grass of the South Dakota Badlands. In the distance, the full moon painted the buttes and mesas in muted pastels.

Behind him, the lights of Rapid City had fallen below the horizon. Below him, two pairs of lights, one red, the other a bluish-white, snaked along the single road that wound its way across the prairie grasslands. Before him was uncertainty. He had no idea which route the fleeing vehicle he tracked would take. He was certain of its destination, however.

He had circled it twice and was convinced that the white sedan that sped along the winding road was in fact the same one he had seen leave the hospital. On his second pass he had seen the vehicle stop. The driver had emerged from the car for a few moments, then returned to the vehicle. It resumed its hasty journey along the desert road.

Farnworth's decision to fly dark proved a wise choice. He didn't want the aircraft's running lights visible to anyone on the ground. He hadn't even filed a flight plan before taking off from the Rapid City Regional Airport. He considered this flight as a covert mission; as covert as the one he wanted to intercept.

Now that he had found his mark, he veered the aircraft away; he could follow at a greater distance to avoid being detected.

In his mind, Farnsworth replayed the whirlwind that was the past forty minutes of quick actions and snap decisions.

The news about the bus crash, along with the possible shootings, had reached Farnsworth quickly. At the same time, he received an anonymous text message about an infant kidnapping at the hospital.

He put two and two together, jumped into his Tesla, and rocketed straight to the hospital maternity ward. There he found a group of panicked parents and screaming babies. An obese nurse was sprawled across the hallway floor. She kept shoving aside another nurse who was trying to calm her and push an oxygen mask onto her face, all the while sobbing and shouting about an army man who stole one of her babies.

Hospital security was also present; along with city police. They had begun their search for the missing infant and its kidnapper and were probably planning to lock down the hospital. Farnsworth left immediately. He had enough information and knew what he had to do next, and that he had precious few minutes to act before the hospital went on lock-down.

He had scrambled down the stairwell and had headed away from where most of the activity was; away from the E.R. and toward the main lobby. He had reached it in time to see two people dressed in boots and black clothing fleeing through the main entrance doors; one of them carrying an infant. He had run to the doors and through the glass had seen the couple placing an infant into a white Subaru sedan. There were some shouts. Doors slammed. Tires screeched as the vehicle took off into the night.

A moan from across the lobby had caught his attention. It was Birchwood; lying on the hard marble floor; immobile. His nose had been smashed and his face a bloody mess; his eyes frozen in a grotesque stare. He could barely speak. A few slurred words managed to pierce through the Colonel's contorted lips; Gordon, Sullivan, Oak Ridge.

If those two were truly heading for Oak Ridge, Tennessee, there were few travel options. Avoiding the interstate, the quickest route was to take route 44, across the Badlands. It was a long shot, but the white sedan would be fairly easy to spot this late at night. It would be one of the few cars on the road. Perhaps the only one.

Farnsworth had dragged Birchwood's body into a corner and propped it in the shadows behind an information kiosk. He did not need the Colonel to be discovered; at least not yet. The fewer clues that the authorities had about the missing infant, the better.

Approaching voices from the adjoining hallway had hastened his pace. He ran out the main doors then circled back to retrieve his Tesla in the parking lot.

With Gordon and Sullivan already having a head start with the infant, he needed to act quickly. Although the Tesla alone could catch them, eventually, a bird's eye view would give him a better chance, even at night; he should be able to spot the vehicle's headlights easily from the air.

His private plane was at the regional airport twenty minutes southeast of Rapid City, off route 44; the same route that he was certain that the fleeing couple would follow. He had called ahead to have an airport mechanic prep his aircraft for immediate takeoff as soon as he arrived.

Once in the air, he was certain that he could catch up with the fleeing couple; and the Neanderthal infant. He had done some quick math in his head. Twenty minutes at seventy-five miles an hour was about 25 miles. That meant the fleeing sedan would pass the airport about five minutes before he arrived. The Cessna's cruising speed was 124 knots; about 140 miles per hour ground speed. He could overtake them in another twenty minutes.

Amazingly, it all worked out. Here he was, forty minutes after leaving the hospital, tracking the car that held the first newborn Neanderthal in over 30,000 years.

The poetic lyrics of the Moody Blue's song returned to his head. He pondered on the last line as he kept his aircraft on a steady course over the pair of dim lights that wound their way along the moonlit grasslands.

We decide which is right, and which is an illusion.

THURSDAY,
6:11 AM CDT

The sun was peeking over the prairie horizon when the vehicle's nav system chirped, indicating that they were nearing the programmed GPS destination. Bob had been driving all night and had stopped at the side of the road twice for the baby's feedings and diaper changes. He needed a strong cup of coffee and a real bathroom break. He sniffed the air.

Someone else needs a bathroom break, too.

He looked over at Mary. She was sound asleep. He looked back at the classified material he was transporting. It was awake and making gurgling noises. He began to smile, but caught himself and looked away. He gently prodded Mary awake.

"Mary? Wake up. I smell something. Mary, do you smell that?"

Mary stretched and yawned, then bolted upright and twisted her body to take a look at the infant. She leaned in toward the child and drew a breath, then pulled back, choking. "Oh, god, yes." She waved at the air in front of her nose. "We need to change a diaper."

"GPS says there's a truck stop or something a few miles ahead. We'll stop there. You can change the baby and I'll check in with the General. We can grab a bite to eat, too."

"Yum. Trucker food." She stuck out her tongue and made a face. "I can't wait."

"You'll live. Can't be any worse than MREs."

"You know, I've never eaten one of those." she confessed.

Bob glanced at her as he kept driving. "What? Not even during basic training? How can you have been in the military all this time and never have eaten an MRE?"

She shrugged. "Don't know. Lucky, I guess. I've always been stationed in city locations, in office buildings."

"Wow. You are lucky. Most everyone gets at least one lousy deployment in some backwater at some time during their service."

"I must be special," she grinned and winked.

A squat collection of buildings appeared on the horizon below the rising sun. "That must be the truck stop," Bob said. "Food for us, diaper and bottle for him." He nodded toward their VIP passenger nestled in the infant carrier behind them.

"He's a she," Mary replied.

"Oh? Okay. I guess I didn't give it much thought."

"Maybe you should change her diaper this time? You need the practice."

Bob looked at her.

She is kidding, I hope.

"I'm sure you can handle this, Lieutenant," he winked.

"Yes, sir," she mock saluted with a grin.

The truck stop's dusty parking lot was sparsely filled with tractor trailers plus a smattering of old pick-up trucks. "I'll change the baby in the ladies room, assuming they have one of those," Mary said. "Then we'll all have some breakfast."

"I'll report in with Holbrooke while you change the baby."

Bob left Mary and the infant at the diner and walked around to the back of the adjacent filling station. He looked around and peered into the windows at the back of the smaller building. Nobody was in sight. He pulled a flip phone from his pocket and punched in a long series of digits. Then he waited. After a few moments General Holbrooke's raspy voice made itself heard.

"Holbrooke."

The digitized, encrypted connection did nothing to improve the voice's intelligibility. Bob strained to listen.

"Captain Gordon reporting, sir. We have the package, sir."

"Good. Did Lieutenant Walker work out?"

"Um, no sir."

"He didn't report for the mission? I'll have his hide!"

"Lieutenant Sullivan assisted me, sir."

"What? I told you. Hell, I ordered you to work with Walker!"

"Birchwood surprised us, sir. I had to move quickly. Plus, Mary knew too much. I couldn't keep her out of the loop."

Should I also tell him that she's the one who figured out when and where Birchwood would strike?

"She shouldn't have been in the loop in the first place," Holbrooke barked. "Is there anything else you need to tell me? Any surprises?"

"None, sir. We successfully intercepted Birchwood after he removed the infant from the maternity ward."

Holbrooke's gravelly tones tumbled through the phone's speaker. "You let Birchwood get to it first? How the hell is that a successful mission?"

"Birchwood is the one on the hospital security cameras stealing the infant, sir. Mary, I mean Lieutenant Sullivan and I then ambushed him as he attempted to leave the hospital with the child. We incapacitated him and left him lying in the hospital lobby. According to news reports, the police and hospital security found him shortly afterwards. He's been arrested and taken into custody for kidnapping."

There was a pause. Bob could hear the General working some phlegm to the top of his throat. There was a cough, then Holbrooke's rough voice returned. "So all the blame is on Birchwood. No one suspects you. Good work, Captain. I knew you could pull this off without a hitch. Where are you now?"

"We're at a truck stop in Holt County, Nebraska, sir. About one half mile west of O'Neill."

"You're following the designated route?"

"Yes, sir."

"Where's Lieutenant Sullivan? She's not there with you, right? She's not listening to this conversation, is she?"

"No, no sir." Bob glanced around. Nobody was in sight. "The Lieutenant is inside with the infant. I'm outside the building."

"You left the Lieutenant alone with it?"

"Um, sir. She's changing its diaper, sir."

Another throat clearing emerged from the phone. "Yes, of course she is. Don't tell the Lieutenant anything about the remainder of this mission. She's not to know that the child is coming here to Oak Ridge. Keep with the cover story that you're delivering the child to a military family that will be foster parents."

"Yes, sir. I have her believing that I don't know the route or final destination, and that I get the next set of travel coordinates only when I report in to you, sir."

"Good, good." There was a pause on the line. "You're not being followed, are you?" the General asked.

"I don't believe so, sir. This route you're having us follow is pretty remote. In fact, this truck stop is the first real sign of civilization we've encountered so far."

"Good. I don't want any more surprises."

"No, sir. No more surprises."

The sound of a click and the flashing cell phone screen told him that the call was terminated.

Bob shoved the phone into his jeans pocket and ambled back to the main building to rejoin Mary and the child.

As he approached the front door, a big rig pulled off the pavement and crossed his path on the unpaved parking lot, kicking up a cloud of dust. He paused and waited for the path to clear and dust to settle.

He entered the diner and scanned the smattering of patrons. Nearly all of them appeared to be overweight, bearded truckers dressed in plaid shirts and jeans. All sat alone. Most were hunkered over their plates of eggs and bacon.

Mary was nowhere to be seen.

She must still be in the ladies room.

He chose an empty booth in the back corner near the restrooms and waited for her and the baby to join him.

Several minutes passed. Bob wondered why Mary was taking so long. The waitress had already delivered coffee and was waiting for their breakfast order.

He checked his watch. Ten minutes had passed.

He was about to get up to check on her when she emerged from the ladies' restroom. She had changed and was now wearing a flowery cotton summer dress. She still had her cowboy boots on.

"You changed." Bob said, not quite knowing whether he was making a statement or posing a question.

"Those jeans were getting too uncomfortable for all this sitting and driving." She placed the infant carrier on the booth's red padded bench seat and settled in behind the table. "Plus, there was a bit of a mess to clean." She winked at the infant who was now awake. Its large blue eyes stared back at Bob.

"I don't think I've heard that baby cry even once," he remarked. "Even with everything it's been through.

"She's my little angel," Mary cooed as she fussed with the infant. "It's time for your bottle, isn't it?"

The waitress reappeared and Mary pulled a baby bottle from the diaper bag's cooler section. "Would you be so kind as to warm this for the little one?" She smiled at the waitress.

Bob watched Mary's eyes follow the waitress until she was out of sight.

She turned to him and asked, "Did you contact the General? Did he tell you anything about the family that is taking her?"

"Um, no," Bob hedged. "The General still hasn't given me that info. He's telling me very little. I don't know where exactly we're driving. I'm certainly not going to ask. All I have are the next set of coordinates."

"Why doesn't he tell us?"

Bob shrugged. "I assume that we don't have need-to-know. We're only couriers at this point, delivering a highly sensitive, top secret package." He nodded at the infant. "We may not even be bringing it to the final destination. The General may be having us hand it off. That might explain why we're only getting our next destination as we report in."

He paused to think.

"This is all happening in real-time, Mary. Whoever we're meeting may also be on the move."

He was watching Mary's eyes as he spoke.

She's getting suspicious. She's not a field-op, but she has a lawyer's mind. She knows how to solve riddles. I'm not sure she's buying all this. I've got to keep her under control.

He smiled at her.

If we screw this up, the General's going to have my hide.

The waitress returned with the baby bottle and took their breakfast order.

Bob stirred his coffee and watched as Mary cradled the infant in her arms and fed it.

She's attached to it. Damn. The General was right. How the hell am I supposed to get them apart now?

THURSDAY, 10:32 AM CDT

Mary awoke with a start. She rubbed her eyes then glanced around. The prairie landscape that had been whizzing by when she fell asleep had been replaced by cornfields.

Bob was next to her, driving. "You were out like a light. Just like the baby. You even drooled on yourself," he chuckled.

She reached up to wipe her chin. It was dry. She slapped him on the shoulder. "You're so mean," she grinned. "What time is it?" She checked her watch then twisted around in her seat. The infant was sleeping in its car seat. "Eat, sleep, poop," she said. "Just like any other kid."

"Especially eat," Bob added. "I've never seen a baby suck down so much formula in one feeding."

"Listen to you, the expert dad."

"Hey. I've had a lot of training. My older sisters did a lot of babysitting when I was growing up. They'd give me a cut for changing the dirty diapers."

"Wait. You're telling me you know how to change a diaper and all this time you've had me doing the dirty work?" She slapped him again. "You sneak, you." She pursed her lips for a moment then broke into a smile and settled back into her seat. The monotonous landscape flowed past. Corn fields. The occasional farmhouse. Silos. More corn fields. "I've never been to this part of the country." She looked around. "It's so … flat."

"Beats being in the Badlands."

"I am impressed by the truck stop diner." She smacked her lips. "That was definitely the best omelet I've ever had. And the waitress was so nice, helping with feeding the baby." She checked her watch again. "How much farther?"

"At least a few hours. I got the next set of GPS coordinates from General Holbrooke while you were sleeping. Just need to follow the directions from the nav system."

"Did he tell you anything about the final destination or the family?"

"No. He's being very cloak and dagger about the whole thing. This is the third set of GPS coordinates that he's given us. Right now we seem to be heading toward the Cumberland Mountain range."

Mary thought about that for a moment.

No, he wouldn't bring the child there. Or would he?

She decided to test him. "Tennessee?" she asked.

"Or Kentucky. Or Northern Mississippi. I can't tell." He glanced over at her and smiled. "Just relax, honey. Enjoy that scenery. Ol' Bob here will take care of everything."

Mary sat staring straight ahead, watching the miles of cornfields slip past them as they drove.

He's hiding something from me. I know he is.

She looked back at Bob. In his sunglasses and polo shirt and with his close-cropped haircut, he could look like any other suburban dad. Well, ... except for maybe the Army Special Forces tattoo on his right bicep. She kept staring at it. It flexed a little as he drove.

She let her eyes wander to his broad, muscular shoulders; his rectangular face and sturdy jaw line.

He glanced over at her.

Embarrassed at being caught, she looked down, then smiled and looked back at him. He was smiling too and reached over to brush away a few strands of her long blonde hair that had slipped down and lay across her face. He pushed them back behind her ear, then he went back to watching the road.

Mary went back to staring at the incessantly repetitive scenery, but her mind was elsewhere, trying to recall an article about a state of the art genomics research center that was somewhere in Tennessee.

She glanced over at his tattoo again. It read DE OPPRESSO LIBER. She worked out the translation in her head.

To free from oppression. That's what I'm doing. I'm freeing this child from oppression.

"You're thinking about something." His voice snapped her back to the moment. "I can almost see the little gears turning in your head."

Mary hesitated. "We're going to Oak Ridge, aren't we?"

He glanced back at her with a look of surprise that disappeared as quickly as the glance itself. "Huh?"

Mary raised her voice a bit. "I said, we're going to Oak Ridge, aren't we?"

"Why do you think that?" His voice sounded a bit tense.

"It just makes sense. All the pieces are coming together."

"I don't know where exactly we're going. Holbrooke seems to have us zig-zagging across the Mid-West." He shrugged. "Why would we go to Oak Ridge? What's there?"

"You know what's there."

She waited for him to come up with an answer.

"If I remember my history correctly, it used to be the headquarters of the Manhattan Project back in WWII," he said. "After that it was an atomic research facility for the federal government, but I think that's been scaled back quite a bit."

"It's still a huge federal research facility."

He shrugged again as if acting perplexed. "Okay. But why would you think we'd be going there? What's this child have to do with atomic energy?"

"Don't you see? They're going to restart the project. Now that they have a living, breathing Neanderthal, they can re-sequence its genes. They'll be able to study her as she grows and develops. They'll learn which genes control which features and can pick and choose the 'Thal characteristics that suit their needs." Mary raised her voice. "They may even use her to breed more. She'll become a 'Thal baby factory!"

Mary could see the corner's of his mouth tighten as he spoke.

"You're not making sense, Mary. The project is over. And besides, why would General Holbrooke

Relic II: Resurrection

have us drive to an old government nuclear research facility?"

"Oh come on now, Bob, I know what's going at Oak Ridge. They have research facilities for a whole range of sciences, including biology. They have a facility dedicated to genomics. It's one of the biggest computational biology research centers in the world."

Bob didn't speak. His eyes remained fixed on the road before them.

"I can't believe you didn't tell me about this!" she said.

Mary studied him. She saw his hands clenching at the steering wheel, but he said nothing. She watched him and waited.

He took a deep breath, exhaled, then said, "You didn't have need-to-know."

Mary exploded. "Oh my god! Really? You're going to hide behind that excuse?" Mary twisted her upper body to face him squarely. The car's shoulder strap slid up across her chest and onto her neck and tangled in her hair. She yanked at it but it locked up. "Damn it!" She pushed herself back into her seat and crossed her arms. "We're getting married for crissakes!"

"Married? What the hell are you talking about, Mary? We're not even engaged."

Mary extended her left hand and examined its bare ring finger. She imagined a princess-cut solitaire set in platinum. "Not yet, but soon."

"Come on, Mary. You're moving way too fast. And did you really believe that we were going to keep this baby?"

"You told me that the project was over. Cancelled."

"It's government property. It's not ours to keep."

"Property?" she shouted. "You think it's property? She's a child and it … she needs a family. We're the reason she exists. And we're the reason her mother is dead. She's our responsibility now and she doesn't deserve to grow up as a science experiment." She paused. "Now I understand why you keep referring to her as 'it'. She has a name. It's Eve."

"You named it?"

"Of course I did."

"Damn it, Mary."

She turned to face him again. "I can't believe you. We just saved this baby's life from that asshole Birchwood, and now you're ready to turn her over to some secret government facility so that they can play god with her genetics."

"Jesus, Mary, it's not ours. It's not our baby."

"It's more ours than anyone else's. Julie's dead. She's dead because of us. Because of our involvement in this crazy secret project. We killed her. We owe it to her, to this child, to raise this child properly. It's our penance. Don't you see? We've sinned. We tried to play God. We've tried to resurrect something that God had deemed unfit to live."

Bob snapped back at her. "In that case, using that logic, we should kill it."

"What the hell are you talking about?"

"It's not a human."

"Then why did they choose Julie, a human female, to carry the child? Why not a chimp or a gorilla? That proves the scientists considered Neanderthals equivalent to humans. She was born of a human. So she is human."

Bob said nothing and kept driving.

Mary turned away, crossed her arms again, and thought for a moment.

He doesn't care about our baby.

She looked at the field of corn that reached nearly up to the edge of the road.

He's going to give it away.

She looked back at the sleeping child. Eve was secure in the car seat.

I can do this.

She took a deep breath, then grabbed the steering wheel and yanked.

"What the hell are you doing, Mary?" Bob shouted as he fought to keep the vehicle on the road.

"She's not a science experiment!" she shouted. "She's a baby."

Despite Mary's yanking at the wheel, Bob managed to regain control of the car. He elbowed her back into her seat. "It's government property, Lieutenant," he barked at her. "And we're following orders."

Mary screamed back at him, "The mission is over."

"The mission was never over, Mary. It's changed ownership."

Mary felt the rage building inside of her. "You lied to me!" she cried out. "You told me that this child would be taken to a safe facility to be raised."

"And it will. But it's also too valuable to not study. The genetic advances alone will be phenomenal. Genomics science can leap years ahead, maybe even decades, based on what we can learn from this child."

Mary grabbed the wheel again and yanked as hard as she could. The car veered to the right and careened into a corn field. They fought for control as the car plowed through the tall green stalks.

A burst of white shoved itself into Mary's face. She wrestled it away. Her heart was pounding and her muscles tense, ready for action.

Bob was hunched forward against the steering wheel. Blood dripped from his face onto the wrinkled mess of white plastic lying in his lap. He groaned. His hands groped for something solid to push himself back into his seat.

Mary grabbed at his seatbelt, wound it once around his neck, wrapped the slack around her forearm and pulled. Bob clawed at the woven belt. His eyes bulged. "Mary!" he gasped. "What are you doing?"

"I'm saving this child." She braced a foot against the center console of the car and gave one last yank. Bob flopped forward, his face buried in the blood stained remnants of his deployed airbag.

The baby was screaming behind her. Mary unbuckled herself and kicked open her door. She moved quickly to free the child from its car seat, and held it close to her breasts. "There, there," she whispered. "It's going to be okay." She coddled and rocked the screaming infant. "Shh. It's okay. You're okay."

While cradling the infant against her chest with one arm, she reached into the rear seat of the damaged vehicle and retrieved the diaper bag along with a backpack filled with formula which she slung over one shoulder.

Mary pushed open the car door and climbed out; one arm curled around the sobbing infant, the other dragging the diaper bag. She looked around and then examined the car. The front of it was mashed against a John Deere combine standing in the partially harvested field. A trail of flattened cornstalks led back to the shoulder of the road.

The distant sound of tractor trailer tires against the coarse road surface worked its way into the otherwise surreal quiet that had descended upon the wreckage.

Mary picked her way through the tangle of ripped-up corn stalks toward the road. She could hear the truck's airbrakes straining as the semi ground to a halt. She reached the edge of the road as the tractor trailer emitted one final snort and its engine stopped. A door slammed shut and a tall, handsome young man about her age came jogging around the front of the cab.

"Hey. You alright," he shouted, apparently overcompensating for the growling diesel engine that he had switched off.

"Yes, we're fine," Mary said as she clambered over the last of the stalks and reached the shoulder of the road.

"What happened?"

"Blew a tire," Mary lied. "Lost control and ended up in the corn field. Hit a combine. That stopped the car but the airbags blew and the radiator's busted."

The truck driver pulled off his cap and scratched his head. His eyes narrowed in the glare of the morning sun.

"It's just me and the baby," she nodded down at the child who had settled down and was now content sucking on the pacifier that Mary had fished out of the diaper bag. She stood, looking at the driver, waiting.

He looked up and down the highway, scratched his head again then replaced his cap. "Well, um, I guess I can give you a lift to the next town," he offered.

"Oh, that would be right sweet of you," Mary said, attempting to speak in what she thought was the local dialect. She smiled. "Then I can call my brother to help pull that wreck of a car out from the corn."

They walked back to the semi. Mary looked up at the climb she'd have to make to get into the cab. She looked back at the driver and extended the swaddled infant to him. "Be a dear, won't you?" she smiled.

He held the infant as Mary hauled herself into the tractor cab, then she reached down and scooped the child from his arms.

She watched as the driver jogged back around the front of the cab and climbed in. She gave him another warm smile then settled back into her seat as the cab shuddered and the tractor's diesel engine roared to life. The airbrakes hissed and snorted as its driver guided the rig back onto the empty road which stretched for miles in front of them.

Mary gazed down at the now sleeping child. "You're so precious," she whispered, and she began to hum a lullaby.

THURSDAY,
12:00 NOON CDT

The blazing noonday sun baked the surrounding corn fields as the big rig thundered along the desolate road. Farnsworth kept a firm grip on the steering wheel as the eighteen-wheeler sped toward the truck stop where he had rented the rig that very morning. His plan was to return the borrowed semi, then fly his Cessna from the O'Neill Municipal Airport back to Rapid City.

He glanced at his wristwatch then tapped at his blue-tooth earpiece, spouted off a string of digits, and waited for the connection to be established. A gruff voice barked back into Farnsworth's ear. He winced.

"Who the hell is this? How did you get this number?" the voice demanded.

"It's Farnsworth."

"Jack? Jack's dead. He's been dead for years. And you're not his son. Junior wouldn't have the balls to call me."

Farnsworth bristled. He detested whenever Grayson referred to his father using the pejorative Junior. Though seething inside, he kept a cool tone. "It's Blake."

"Blake? Jack's grandson? You mean that piano playing pansy? The one who used to act and take dance lessons?"

Farnsworth rolled his eyes. "You remember me, Grayson."

"How could I forget? Jack had such high hopes for you. He imagined you taking the reins of the company one day. Ha! Fat chance of that happening. Especially now. The company is in ruins."

Farnsworth smiled to himself. "I know. I was the one who did all that."

Grayson's strident voice filled Farnsworth's ear. "What? What the fuck are you talking about? What did you have to do with the feds raiding the company and uncovering the cloning project?"

"Who do you think leaked the info?"

"Don't jerk me around. I know who it was. It was Summerston. That idiot scientist leaked out all the data from the secret lab in the desert. And using Morse code, no less. Clever bastard. But still a bastard. What the hell did you have to do with it?"

"Who do you think put the plan into action? Got the ball rolling?"

"You? Ha! No fucking way. You couldn't even act that part, much less actually do it for real."

Farnsworth spoke in low tones. "Summerston may have leaked the info, but he leaked it into the ether. He had no idea who, if anyone, was going to hear his radio signal. Even if they did, who the hell was going to believe his story?"

"So, you're the one who posted that stuff on the internet? On that stupid writer's website?"

"Yes, that was me. I was also the one who drove out into the desert and uncovered the location of the secret research facility where Summerston was being held."

Grayson's tone calmed a bit. "So, what do you want?"

"I want my grandfather's company."

"If you haven't noticed, you smart ass, you're grandfather's company is in the shitter."

"I also want the money to rebuild it."

Grayson laughed. "Money? Why the fuck would I give you any money? Besides, you already got your inheritance from Jack. My attorneys tried like hell to take back that dough. Jack was a real genius the way he locked up that trust fund so that no one could get their fingers on it. But now it's all yours. What other money are you talking about?"

"Cut the crap, Grayson. I know you have a stash in the Cayman Islands."

"Well, well. The little actor boy can talk tough. I guess those acting lessons are finally coming in handy, eh?"

"I had a very good teacher. You remember Caldwell?"

"The head of F&G security?"

"Yeah, that guy. I spent some time working in his department. Got some very useful training. I paid very close attention to him. He was fascinating. A real throwback to mid-twentieth century corporate culture."

"Okay. Big deal, Farnsworth. So you picked up a little street smarts. What of it?"

"My grandfather wanted me to take the company back from you. He felt betrayed by you, the way you stole the company from him slowly, piece by piece."

"Your grandfather was a smart guy. A genius of a scientist. But he sucked as a businessman. He needed me to run everything. I'm the one who built that company."

"And I'm the one who took it down."

Farnsworth winced again as Grayson's shouting ripped through the earpiece. "So, you're rubbing my face in it now? Is that what this call is all about? Christ, you really are a pansy. You couldn't even come to me face to face. You have to do it behind a cell phone."

Farnsworth paused for effect. "What if I told you I had a way to rebuild the company."

There was a moment of silence before Grayson responded. "What the heck are you blabbing about? F&G will never recover from what you did to it."

"I have an asset that will raise the company from the dead."

"I'm not sure any amount of money could do that. We'll need investors, stockholders, and sharp scientists with vision and passion. There's no way that we'll attract that type of wealth and talent back to the company. Not after the shit you pulled."

"What if I told you that I have one of the babies?"

There was a pause on the line. "Say that again."

"I have one of the 'Thal infants."

There was another pause on the line before Grayson fired back. "That's bullshit. How did you get possession of one? And how did it come to exist in the first place. I don't recall that we ever successfully implanted any of the zygotes that Summerston had created."

Farnsworth downshifted the rig as it approached a slow moving pick-up truck. The engine growled with the change of gears.

"What's that noise, Farnsworth? Where the hell are you?"

"Doesn't matter where I am. What does matter is where you want to be."

"You're full of shit, playboy. If you really had a 'Thal, and any brains, you'd be offering it up on OpenBazaar or one of the other Dark Net sites."

"Not only do I have a 'Thal, I have a female. I'm sure you know what that's worth. You can use it to start breeding another generation."

Another pause. A long one this time. Farnsworth could almost hear Grayson's mind scheming. "I'm offering you the chance to rebuild F&G," Farnsworth said into his earpiece.

"I want proof. Not just photos. I want cell samples, DNA. Not just the reports, I want viable specimens, cell cultures."

"Not a problem. All that can be arranged. What I want to see is a down payment. Something to show that you're serious, and that you can play."

"You're insulting me, Farnsworth. You know I'm good for it."

Ha! He's starting to beg.

"Time to ante-up. I'll give you forty eight hours. After that, I will put the 'Thal for sale on a Dark Net site. I'm sure I'll find a buyer."

"Don't try to strong-arm me you son-of-a-bitch. You know the connections I have. I want that 'Thal. And you're gonna give it to me."

"Forty eight hours, Grayson. You have this number."

Farnsworth tapped at his earpiece, terminating the call. He pulled the trucker's cap from his head and tossed it onto the dashboard. Through the semi's expansive windshield he saw the empty road ahead of him. Next to him, safely strapped in its car seat was a sleeping infant. Mary was seated on the other side, slouched against the passenger door of the big rig's cab. A half-finished bottle of water was slowly slipping from her fingers' grip as her body sank deeper into a drug induced slumber.

Farnsworth smiled and put his eyes back on the road that stretched before him. It was clear to the horizon.

ABOUT THE AUTHOR

Jonathan has been "on the run" for some time, after exposing a covert and ethically questionable military project to breed super soldiers.

The facts behind the fiction of this project are revealed in the first novella *Relic*. Disturbingly close to the truth, *Relic* describes a world in which human soldiers are replaced with something much deadlier, and much more uncontrollable, with consequences that could spell the end of humanity as we know it.

Jonathan Brookes is known to have spent the last thirty years weaving his way through one high tech company after another, leaving a trail of cancelled projects, failed mergers and corporate bankruptcies. He was last seen on a wooded trail between the Melville Nauheim Shelter and The Greenwood Lodge and Campsite on Route 9, near Big Pond, Woodford, VT.

His current whereabouts are unknown....

Books by author **Gregory S. Lamb**
http://gslambpdxauthor.webs.com

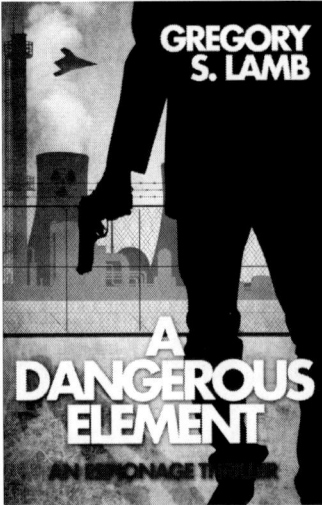

A Dangerous Element

An American covert
operation to destroy the
nuclear enrichment
program at Natanz, Iran
goes bad when a virus is
discovered in the facility's
closed control network.
Former combat pilot,
Colonel Mark "Coolhand"
Reynolds holds the key to
unraveling the cast of
shady characters involved
in the operation and cover
up.

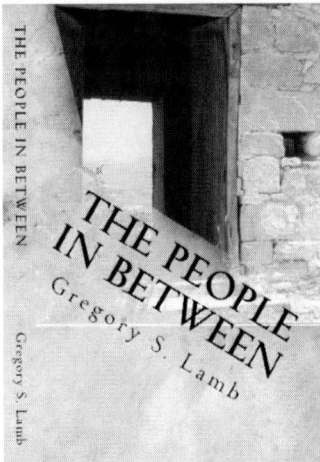

The People In Between

Kiraz Nora Johansson and
her twin brother never
knew their mother who
died while giving birth.
By invitation of a family
friend she travels to
Cyprus and discovers her
family's past. Through a
history that was nearly
lost to her and her
troubled brother, she
learns what it means to
love and becomes forever
tied to the Cypriot people
and their unforgettable
island home.

Books by author Roland Hughes
http://johnsmith-book.com/

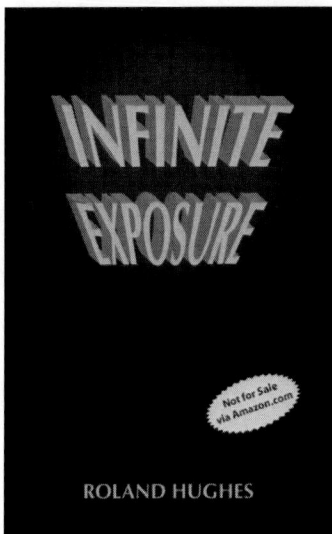

Infinite Exposure

An espionage novel written in 2008, the author has predicted stories that are now in today's news headlines! This heavily researched work of fiction was written shortly after 9/11 and long before identity theft or data breaches were in the news.

Read and decide for yourself which is scarier, what it says is coming or how much it has already gotten right?

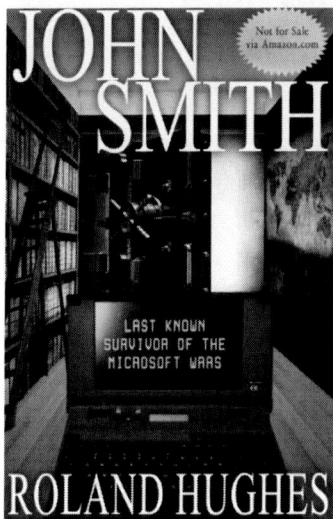

John Smith

John Smith – Last Known Survivor of the Microsoft Wars' is a work of dystopian fiction some reviewers have declared as important as George Orwell's '1984' and Aldous Huxley's 'Brave New World'. John Smith is the last survivor. He is the only one left with knowledge of Earth that was; an Earth that didn't have 12 continents.

Books by author Jeffrey Allen Mays

http://jeffreyallenmays.com/

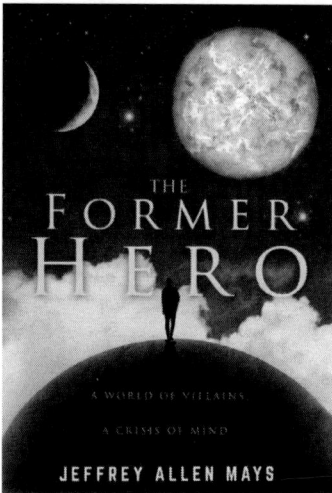

The Former Hero
Winner of the 2015 Book
Award for the Texas
Authors Association.

In a city controlled by
corporate villains, the lives
of four troubled souls
become intertwined in the
search for a young daughter
feared abducted by the
burgeoning sex trade. Each
finds they are on their own
journey not only of self-
discovery but in the aching
questions about life. This
multi-genre thriller is a
literary feast.

Books by author Oliver F. Chase

http://oliverchase.wordpress.com/

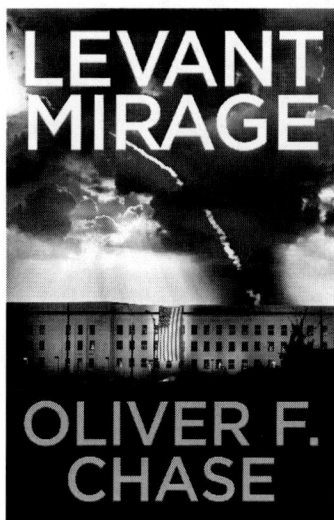

<u>*Levant Mirage*</u>
After fifteen centuries of religious conflict, the world faces a grave choice–submit to the demands of terrorists or face mass obliteration. America declassifies a top secret PhD dissertation and a disgraced soldier becomes hated and feared by both friends and enemies. As society crumbles under the weight of hateful demands, a handful of world citizens gamble their lives and their treasure in a last, desperate attempt to save civilization from an act threatening to reset the clock by a thousand years.

Books by author Jeffrey Moore

http://www.jefferyemoore.com/

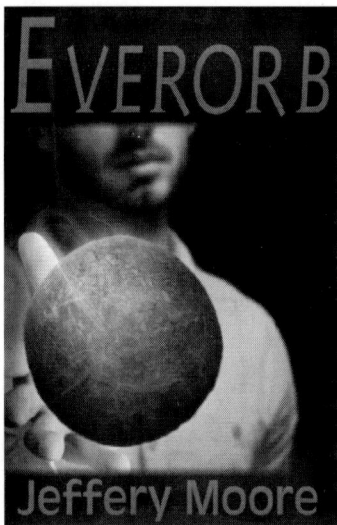

Everorb
Nightmares ruined Trent Michaels' life. Punk kid, drug addict, convicted killer, and mental patient, he's being kicked to the street, ill-equipped to deal with his dreams. A transition program offers him an unexpected chance at salvation. Powerful, desperate people struggle to find out what he knows about Atlas, a relic revealed only in his nightmares. Channeling his dreams, Trent pursues Atlas and in doing so, rebuilds his sanity and exposes supernatural abilities.

The Fact Behind the Fiction!

Read the original story spun around the secrets
revealed by microgenomist Dr. Frank Summerston.

Relic
by Jonathan Brookes
http://jonathanfbrookes.wordpress.com/

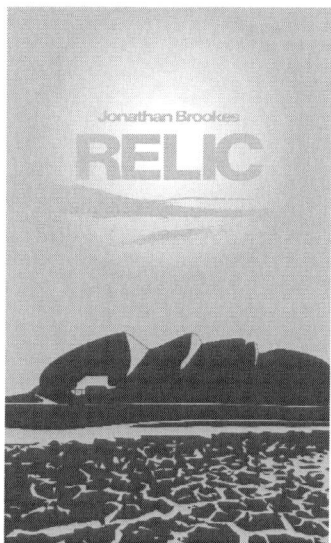

Warfare has entered a new era. The cold war is long over. Battleships, bombers, and tanks, the big iron of twentieth century military might, have taken a back seat to unmanned drones, IEDs, and suicide bombers.

Fueled by cutting edge biotechnology, in a world where Dr. Strangelove politics and Jurassic Park science collide, the military embarks on a desperate project to seek out and destroy enemy combatants on their home turf.

Made in United States
North Haven, CT
21 October 2025